the Healing Summer

the Healing Summer

Heather B. Moore

Mirror Press

Copyright © 2021 by Heather B. Moore
Hardcover edition
All rights reserved
No part of this book may be reproduced in any form whatsoever without prior written permission of the publisher, except in the case of brief passages embodied in critical reviews and articles. This is a work of fiction. The characters, names, incidents, places, and dialog are products of the author's imagination and are not to be construed as real.
Interior design by Cora Johnson
Edited by Joanne Lui, Lorie Humpherys, and Alice Shepherd
Cover design by Rachael Anderson
Cover image credit: Deposit Photos 214783142
Published by Mirror Press, LLC
ISBN: 978-1-952611-27-8

OTHER BOOKS BY HEATHER B. MOORE

The Paper Daughters of Chinatown
Prosperity Ranch Series
Pine Valley Series
Love is Come
Condemn Me Not

Dedicated to:

My aunts who are wonderful women I look up to.

Becki Strasser, Ann Herman, Ronnalynn Dean,

Edith Brown, Beverly Brown, and Toni Oblad

The Healing Summer

Summer, 1981

At the age of ninety-four, Maggie Howard's final wish is to return to San Francisco and find out what happened to the young man who saved her life in 1906 after the disastrous earthquake and fires that devastated the city. They'd been trapped beneath a collapsed roof for hours, injured and unable to call for help.

The morning of their rescue, Orlando Gallo promised he would find her again. But Maggie hasn't seen or heard from him in over seventy years, and now, widowed and childless, Maggie hopes to leave her estate to Orlando's descendants. She invites her neighbor, forty-year-old Jo Sampson, to travel with her, and as the two women return to San Francisco to track down Orlando, they form a strong bond of friendship and healing that transcends time and place.

Chapter One

Seattle
Summer, 1981

Jo Sampson knew life could always be worse. Logic—plus an MFA and doctorate in history—told her that life was often worse. Yet, today made her top five list of worst days.

"Mo-om." Alec's thirteen-year-old voice cracked as he called to her from the bottom of the stairs.

Jo had brought the large white envelope upstairs to her bedroom to open in privacy. But she'd forgotten to shut the door, so her solitude had ended before she could finish reading through the copy her lawyer had sent of her final, signed divorce papers.

"The taxi's going to leave," Alec hollered. "I'm getting in with or without you. I'll call you from a pay phone when I get to the airport."

If it had been any other day, when Jo's divorce papers weren't a glaring white rectangle on the new violet bedspread she'd bought after Liam moved out, she might have laughed at her son's declaration.

"I'm coming." Jo hoped the tremble didn't sound in her voice. "I'm coming," she whispered to herself as she slipped the papers into the envelope. She already knew what they said, and what did it matter, anyway?

Her fourteen-year marriage was officially over.

Today, she'd drop her son at the airport to spend the summer with his dad and Liam's new fiancée in their new home in San Diego, where Alec would meet his new puppy...

New. New. New.

Jo didn't like all this *new*.

And she didn't really like her son flying so far on his own, but Alec had said he'd be fine. Liam said he'd be fine. So Jo had to live with it.

A soft snore came from the end of the bed. Speaking of old versus new. Jo had been left with the old dog—Sadie—and the old house. One hundred years old, to be exact. The house, not the dog.

When she'd first awakened this morning, hovering in the gray area between sleep and wakefulness, for several blessed seconds, she hadn't remembered all the changes in her life. Then the ache in her heart began before her brain even comprehended the changes of the past four months and three days.

Jo blinked away the burning in her eyes as she heard the front door open, and Alec holler another threat as his suitcase made that clickety-clack sound across the porch.

"Happy birthday to me," Jo whispered.

Sadie lifted her head for a moment, her sleepy eyes seeming to say, "Sorry you're not having a good birthday." But then her eyes slipped closed, and the snores started again. Sadie was ten, but she acted like she was fifty.

Releasing a sigh, Jo turned from the white envelope on the bed, and the sleeping dog, and left her bedroom. As she descended the stairs, she tried not to think of the hours and hours she and Liam had spent upgrading this one-hundred-year-old house. She loved everything about it, from the new banister, to the refinished hardwood floor, to the paint colors of Arctic Cotton and Misty Surf she'd chosen, to the chandelier she'd found at a swap meet hanging in the front entrance.

Jo grabbed her purse from the hall table, refinished only last summer when she was living a different life—a life she had no part of now. She walked through the open front door, and indeed, Alec was making good on his promise.

He had the trunk of the taxi open and was lifting his suitcase into it. His face had reddened, and his muscles strained. What in the world had he packed?

"Let me help you," Jo called to him. She locked the front door, then hurried to help her son.

Surprisingly, he waited for her, instead of proceeding with his usual stubbornness to do everything himself.

Jo grasped one side of the suitcase and lifted, then groaned. "What did you put in this?"

Alec pushed up the black-framed glasses on his nose. The gesture was so like Liam that a pang shot through Jo. Alec also resembled Liam, with his sandy-brown hair and studious green eyes. Jo had first noticed Liam's eyes when she met him in a faculty meeting at Seattle Central College.

"I want to show Dad my geode collection," Alec said in that no-nonsense tone he'd perfected.

Of course, he does. Liam was a science teacher, and Alec's interests were heading in that direction, too. "You know the weight limit is fifty pounds on the plane?"

"You can bring something heavier," Alec informed her. "They put on a tag and charge extra. Mrs. Howard told me."

Leave it to Alec to ask for advice from their world-traveling neighbor, Maggie Howard. Jo decided she was too tired to argue with her son about the wisdom of hauling rocks on a plane ride. "All right, lift on three."

Once the suitcase was inside the trunk of the car, Jo said, "Don't you want to say goodbye to Sadie?"

"I already did," Alec said. "When you were in the shower."

At least there was that. Alec was still loyal to his dog—a dog that Jo remembered finding with Liam. Another memory she'd have to stuff away. She rerouted herself back to the present and greeted the taxi driver, an older woman who had more colors in her hair than Jo could identify.

"There's Mrs. Howard," Alec said as they pulled onto the street.

Jo looked over to see their elderly neighbor out walking in her slow gait. Maggie Howard was a quiet woman, but she faithfully walked the neighborhood each day. The sight always inspired Jo to exercise herself—another goal she was determined to achieve this summer.

Jo and Alec waved as they passed the woman and Mrs. Howard waved back, her eyes as sharp as ever. The few times Jo had visited Maggie's home, she had been impressed with the woman's collection of art. Everything from seascapes to miniature portraits from sixteenth-century Europe decorated the woman's walls.

Maggie's husband had been an innovator of dental implants, and he'd traveled the world presenting at medical conferences. Maggie went along and collected art. A charmed life, if there ever was one, Jo decided.

The taxi continued out of the neighborhood, and the driver kept up a friendly and steady chatter with Alec as they drove to the Seattle airport.

Jo felt grateful for the driver's distraction because the reality of Alec's leaving was starting to settle in. She'd already determined not to cry at the airport—after Alec had made her promise, of course. Besides, having her son away for the summer would theoretically allow Jo plenty of time to work on that historical study about Mongol queens she'd started three years ago. The research had been fascinating, but with everyone home during the summers—Liam was on the same professor schedule—writing had always taken a back seat.

No more delays, Jo determined, trying not to feel the impact of the reason *why* she'd now finally have so much uninterrupted time. Alec would be gone, and her marriage was over.

"Which terminal?" the taxi driver asked.

Before Jo could answer, Alec did it for her.

As the driver pulled to the curb, the impact that Alec would really be leaving, and the time was now, made Jo's eyes sting.

"You're not going to cry, are you, Mom?" Alec said from the back seat.

Jo dragged in a breath. "Of course, not," she said in a cheerful, albeit wobbly, tone. She was probably not even fooling the taxi driver. She popped open her door and told the driver, "Maybe you'll be my return trip home."

As it turned out, Jo reemerged from the airport an hour-and-a-half later, when she knew Alec's plane had left the ground. After her tears had dried, she'd called Liam from a pay phone to let him know that the flight was on time, and only when he confirmed he'd be there to pick up Alec did she leave the terminal to find another taxi.

Jo would have driven, but her car was in the shop. Her second taxi driver of the day was a young man, twenty-something, who talked about his hobby of painting miniature board game creatures. Jo had never heard of such a thing and wanted to ask Liam about it. But then she remembered. She couldn't ask Liam. Well, it would be very awkward if she did. It wasn't like they were enemies, but they weren't really friends, either. Not anymore.

"It's not you, it's me," Liam had told her on that rainy day in early February. "Things have been off between us for a while. I don't feel myself anymore, and you don't deserve half a husband."

Jo had wanted to ask him what he meant by "a while," but she was too numb to ask those types of questions. He moved out the week before Valentine's Day, and on Valentine's night, while Jo was on her second bowl of ice cream, Alec had called her from Liam's apartment, where he was spending the weekend, and asked her why Dad had taken another woman to dinner.

On Liam's parenting weekend, he'd gone on a date and left Alec home alone. Jo had then known the truth about Liam's leaving her.

When the taxi turned onto her street, Jo realized she'd tuned out whatever the driver had been speaking about in the last ten minutes. When he pulled into her driveway, she thanked him and paid, then climbed out.

Now, her summer was about to begin, and as she walked up the steps to her front door, she decided that today, she could review her manuscript pages. Then tomorrow, she'd go to the library to do research after she got her car out of the shop.

Since today was her birthday, she'd order pizza for dinner. Weren't fortieth birthdays supposed to be a bigger deal than normal? She'd order the kind of pizza *she* liked, and not the kind she always ordered for Liam and Alec to make them happy. It wasn't like she had a group of girlfriends to go out with. Any co-workers had been Liam's friends to begin with. Jo had just been the wife. Besides, it was hard to pin down any of their colleagues in the summer.

Jo and Liam. Liam and Jo. They always got smiles about the combination of their names. Now, it was just *Jo.* And *Liam and Krista.*

The Healing Summer

Jo told herself she would be happy with the homemade card and hand-me-down Rubik's Cube from Alec. It was sweet of him to give it to her. He had two others, but he'd said that his first was his favorite. And she couldn't really expect a thirteen-year-old kid to go out and get her a gift on his own. That would have been what Liam and Alec did together.

When she unlocked the front door and stepped into the house, the empty quiet was like a blow to her stomach. She shut the door with a quiet click, then stood in the entryway and listened to the clock hanging above the bottom stairs ticking. She couldn't remember the last time the house had been quiet enough to hear the ticking of a clock.

The memory of when she had bought the clock flashed through her mind. She and Liam had been at an antique store in downtown Seattle, and they'd browsed the store together, walking hand in hand. Jo had pulled Liam to a stop when she saw the clock—the Roman numerals against the mosaic background had practically yelled at her to take notice.

"Buy it," Liam had said, squeezing her hand.

"I don't dare look at the price," Jo told him.

She held her breath as Liam reached for the hanging white tag and turned it over. "Three-hundred and fifty."

Jo sighed. "Too much."

Liam released her hand, grasped the clock with both hands, and took it down from its spot on the wall. "Happy anniversary, sweetheart." He leaned close and kissed her.

Now, Jo closed her eyes. How long ago had that been? Five years? *Six?* She leaned against the front door, not wanting to walk farther into the house. Every item and every room would bring back another memory. Jo imagined herself by the end of the night lying on the floor, beneath the weight of too many memories. All of them had been tainted now.

Liam had fallen in love with another woman, and here Jo

stood alone in the entryway of her beautiful home. Feeling as empty as the house.

When a knock sounded at the door, Jo startled.

Heart pounding, she swallowed back her surprise, then checked the peephole. Seconds later, Jo pulled the door open, a forced smile on her face, as she greeted her neighbor, Maggie Howard.

Chapter Two

MAGGIE DECIDED THAT JO Sampson looked as if she'd seen a ghost.

"I'm not dead yet," Maggie said.

Jo blinked, and her smile faltered. Yet her voice was perfectly sweet when she replied, "Hello, Maggie. What brings you here today?"

Maggie wasn't fooled for a moment. This woman had been crying, and by the looks of it, she needed a square meal. Or three. Her long, brunette hair was pulled into a high ponytail, and her normally warm brown eyes looked dull. "I've come to give you a birthday present."

The brown face of a dog nudged between Jo and the doorframe. "Hello, Sadie," Maggie said promptly. This family had the most mellow dog in the county, and Maggie wondered if the creature ever barked.

Jo patted Sadie's head, then met Maggie's gaze. "I . . . How did you know it was my birthday?" Jo raised her dark brows. She was one of those women who wore her emotions on her face.

Maggie had learned a long time ago to hide her regrets and painful memories. It was better that way. She couldn't bear the look of pity in another person's eyes when they learned all that Maggie had suffered.

Goodness, the woman looked as if she were about to cry. "Never mind that." Maggie didn't want to admit that she remembered dates and events all too well. The good along with the bad. "You're forty? A girl's fortieth birthday can't go by without a celebration, right?"

"Right," Jo said in a faint voice.

Sadie plopped down at Jo's feet, a bored expression on her face.

Maggie refocused on Jo. The woman really needed a few days in the sun—maybe at the beach, although the Washington shoreline wasn't the warmer Californian beach. Maggie pushed any thoughts of California from her mind—for now. There would be plenty of time later, when she was alone, to indulge in those old memories.

"I'm taking you to dinner," Maggie continued. "And you're driving."

The smile that spread on Jo's face was genuine. At last. "I'm driving, huh?" Then her smile dimmed. "Except my car's in the shop. I had to take Alec to the airport in a taxi earlier."

Maggie nodded. She'd seen the taxi, and that forlorn look on Jo's face. It was what had prompted her to put this plan together. "We can take Herb," she said. "He hasn't been out in a while."

"You still have your Lincoln?"

"That I do," Maggie said. "Although they took away my license, it doesn't mean I had to give up my car, too."

"Okay," Jo said, her tone sounding brighter.

Maggie had done the right thing after all. "Are you available in about an hour? Herb doesn't like to deal with traffic."

Jo smiled at that.

"And once it gets dark," Maggie continued, "I like to be home sipping my orange tea."

Jo looked as if she might say no, but then she said, "All right. Do you have a place in mind?"

"Well, it's *your* birthday, but I do love Italian," Maggie said. "Have you tried Bello's?"

"I haven't, is it new?" Jo asked.

"No, it's been there since the sixties." Maggie really shouldn't torture herself by going there again, but she was like a moth flying straight toward a flame.

Jo nodded. "How fancy is this place?"

"Fancy," Maggie said. "Dress up."

Moments later, when Maggie was making her slow way back to her neighboring home, she found that she was smiling to herself. Nights out were rare for her, and at age ninety-four, she didn't dare drive herself. That, and the fact she'd lost her license three years ago. Couldn't pass the driving test. The Parkinson's medication she took compromised her reaction time should someone suddenly brake in front of her.

Maggie stopped when another neighbor's cat streaked across her path. "What are you up to, Sergeant?" she called after the gray tabby. The cat didn't respond but continued to the other side of the road. She and Bruce had never had pets on account of Bruce's allergies. Maybe she should get a cat or a dog now.

She turned up the walk to her stately two-story home. She'd lived here most of her married life, and she still remembered the day she and her husband bought it.

"I'd give you the world if I could, Maggie," Bruce had said. "But this house will have to do."

Maggie had laughed and hugged him. The house represented all her dreams for the future, hoping the five bedrooms would soon be filled with children, laughter, and love. But the children had never come. Only miscarriages.

After the seventh miscarriage, Bruce had sat her down on their pristine couch. Told her he wanted his wife back, that he loved her whether or not they had children, and he was going to take her to his next convention in Europe.

When Maggie had packed for the trip, she felt as if she were packing away her dreams of having children. Buckling up her suitcase had brought finality to her hope of becoming a mother. By the time she stepped off the plane in Paris, she'd reconciled herself to her new life. She hadn't expected to be so charmed by the museums of Europe. While Bruce met with medical experts, Maggie had visited museums, libraries, antique shops, and gift boutiques.

Her first art purchase was a painting of the French seashore at dawn. The artist had captured the pinks and golds of the early dawn light as it reflected off the sea. She'd never heard of the painter, but the shop owner said that he was well-known throughout Europe.

Maggie opened the door to her house and made a beeline for the kitchen. The walk to Jo's had winded her for some reason, and she needed some restorative tea. Or perhaps she was feeling faint because of the anticipation of asking Jo something important over dinner. If Jo turned her down, then Maggie didn't know what she would do.

She set a teakettle of water on the stove, then waited for the water to boil. Maggie didn't mind living alone for the most part. Bruce had been gone for years, and her only regret was her oldest regret—no children, no little Bruces or Maggies. And as a result, no grandchildren. Bruce had amassed a sizable fortune, and upon his death, Maggie had found she had no personal use for it. She continued to donate to her favorite charities and even bought a few more paintings. But shopping from catalogs was not the same thing as wandering through antique shops in Budapest or Liverpool.

The teakettle hissed, and Maggie removed it, then poured the hot water into a porcelain mug. Next, she added a tea bag of her favorite variety. She enjoyed the sweet flavor of the orange, and she always added cinnamon and honey to make it more robust.

The Healing Summer

Maggie took her time sipping her tea before reaching for the scrapbook she'd been adding to over the years. She'd shown it to Bruce once early in their marriage when it had only been about twenty pages long, and she found that answering his questions about her young life had only brought her more heartache.

If she kept her memories to herself, she could hold them close, and live a life beyond the pain.

If she shared her past, the pain grew and grew until she felt as if she were drowning.

But every year on the anniversary of her last day in San Francisco, she allowed herself an afternoon of going through the scrapbook. She hadn't added to it since Bruce's death. She wasn't sure why. Perhaps it was because she felt if she were to put anything into a scrapbook, it should include things about Bruce and their life together.

Since today was the anniversary of the day she'd left San Francisco for good, she'd indulge in looking at the pages again. She wondered how many more times she'd do this. Ninety-four years of age was nothing to sniff over, and she had no idea how much longer she'd live. Months? Years? More and more people were living into their nineties, yet Maggie couldn't expect that *he* was still alive. If he were, he'd be the remarkable age of ninety-six, for he'd been two years older than Maggie's nineteen when she'd met him that fateful day of April 18, 1906.

Orlando Gallo.

Just thinking his name sent a warm shiver along Maggie's arms. Could he still be alive? Did he still remember her? Surely, he had dozens of grandchildren and possibly great-grandchildren. Italians always had large families; it was almost a religion.

Maggie wondered whom Orlando had married. Was she

Italian? Did they stay in San Francisco? Did he ever become a famous artist? At least in his own right?

Maggie could admit that her interest in art had begun with Orlando. She could also admit that she'd been disappointed time and time again when she'd written to art galleries, first in San Francisco, then throughout the state and other surrounding states, inquiring if they'd ever heard of an artist by the name of Orlando Gallo.

Every response she'd received had been in the negative.

So, she was left to wonder all these years.

When she'd met with her estate manager last week, an idea had formed. What if she tracked down Orlando's descendants and left her estate to them? They could divide up the money from the trust fund and the sale of the home. It would be her way to thank Orlando for saving her life. But then the doubts set in. She was ninety-four. She couldn't very well drive herself down the Pacific coast. How would she find a man from seventy years ago? He could be dead. He could have moved across the country. Maybe he'd never married at all.

But the idea had kept Maggie awake at night. She had to try, and tonight, she'd present her plan to Jo. And God willing, Jo would agree to help Maggie find Orlando.

Chapter Three

JO CHOSE THE DARK green dress she'd worn to the winter faculty dinner. She loved the soft rayon fabric and the way the shoulder pads made her waist seem slimmer than it was. The dress was perhaps a winter color, but she could wear her black heeled sandals. Besides, the clouds were already gathering for the promised rainstorm. She hoped that Maggie, *and Herb*, weren't opposed to driving in the rain, because Jo found she was looking forward to this birthday outing.

Who would have thought on her last birthday, when she and her husband and son had gone to dinner and then hung out in a downtown bookstore, that she'd be spending this birthday with their elderly neighbor? Jo reached for her makeup bag and applied a dark mauve lipstick, then fastened gold hoop earrings in her earlobes. There. She hoped Maggie would be pleased.

Jo walked downstairs, ignoring the sound of the ticking clock this time. She was finished with tears for the day.

She found Sadie waiting in the kitchen, standing patiently over her food bowl. She'd always been a mellow dog and was so tolerant of Alec's antics over the years. Right now, the dog looked a bit downcast.

"Missing your buddy?" Jo said, giving the dog's back a

good rub. "Me, too." She fed her and set out fresh water as well.

Then Jo headed outside in the drizzle, locking up the house.

Maggie was ready and even had the garage door open where she stood in front of the Lincoln. The woman always looked classy. She wore a floral brocade jacket over a soft white blouse, with an A-line navy skirt and low-heeled pumps. Like a true lady, Maggie wore nude-colored hose. She'd also applied a dusting of rouge, pale pink lipstick, and penciled-in brows, which brought more attention to her blue-green eyes.

"You look lovely," Jo told her.

"Thank you," Maggie said. "And so do you."

Jo smiled, her heart feeling lighter with each passing moment. The maroon Lincoln looked as if it had been spit-polished, and the color gleamed beneath the garage light.

The two women climbed into the car after Maggie said she didn't need any help, and Jo started the Lincoln. She'd never driven such a large car before, so she backed out slowly, then pulled onto the street.

As they drove, Maggie asked a few questions about Alec, and Jo found it nice to talk about her son to someone who knew him.

"He's such a smart boy," Maggie said. "I've enjoyed watching him grow up."

The wistful tone in her voice was obvious. Maggie had once told Jo that after a series of miscarriages, she'd given up on the idea of having children with Bruce.

When they reached the restaurant, Jo realized she was quite hungry, and she was also pleased to see the place didn't look crowded. They parked, and Jo and Maggie walked to the entrance. Inside, the décor was charming, reminiscent of what Jo supposed a real Italian restaurant might look like, complete with red-and-white checkered tablecloths and interior brick walls.

Low, classical music played as their hostess led them to a table. Only two other tables in the restaurant were occupied.

To Jo's surprise, Maggie spoke Italian when their waitress showed up a few moments later with ice water. When the waitress left, Maggie said, "Greta has been my waitress a few times."

"You speak Italian?" Jo asked.

Maggie smiled. "I've picked some up over the years. Comes in handy when traveling."

"I'm impressed." Languages weren't really Jo's strength, although she enjoyed learning to pronounce things.

Maggie reached for the glass of water the waitress had brought, her hands trembling. She took a sip, then set it down. "I've tried everything on this menu. All you need to tell me is what kind of dish you like, and I'll be able to recommend a few things."

"All right." Jo looked down at the menu. The prices were about double compared to any other restaurant she'd been to. She scanned the names of the dishes, and most of them she was familiar with since Italian food had become an American staple. "I'm sure it's all wonderful. Maybe one of the lasagnas? I didn't know there were so many different kinds."

"Do you like mushrooms?"

Jo nodded.

"Then, I'd recommend the Portobello mushroom lasagna," Maggie said. "And it goes wonderfully with a red wine."

The dinner bill would be a fortune if they ordered wine. Plus, Jo wasn't sure how to gauge the potency, and if she was driving, it was probably better to stick with water. "No wine for me," she told Maggie. "Water's perfect."

Maggie's penciled brows lifted. "If you don't mind, I'd like to have a glass of wine with my dinner. Get my courage up."

Jo smiled. "Courage for what?" When Maggie's face flushed, Jo's curiosity was piqued. The woman was always so composed, so confident, that it made Jo wonder what she could be nervous about.

"I'll explain after our food comes."

Greta returned and took their orders, and while Jo burned with questions, she held up her end of the conversation as she told Maggie about the history classes she taught at Seattle Central. She didn't mention how Liam was now engaged to the woman he'd left Jo for. Maggie didn't ask about Liam. In fact, they didn't speak of the divorce at all.

It was refreshing, Jo decided, to speak about adult things without going *there*.

When their food came, Maggie was in the middle of telling Jo about a trip to Denmark. Jo had kept her envy at a minimum, thinking that maybe if she stayed strict with her personal finances, she might one day travel, too.

But now she needed to pay attention to the lasagna on her plate. Steam rose from the layers of cheese, mushrooms, and pasta. The first bite convinced her food could be ambrosia, and the second bite convinced her that the restaurant was worth every penny.

"What do you think?" Maggie asked from across the table.

Jo looked up, and Maggie chuckled, probably because Jo had practically moaned in pleasure at the taste.

"It's wonderful."

Maggie lifted her glass of red wine. "To good Italian food and neighbors with birthdays."

Jo laughed. She hadn't even had any wine, yet the delicious food was its own blissful therapy. She lifted her water glass. "To neighbors who have working cars and know the best places to eat."

The two women clinked glasses and smiled at each other. At that moment, the earlier grief of the day faded, and something new and warm pricked Jo's heart. She'd never viewed Maggie as any more than a kind neighbor who was patient with Alec's questions, but now, Jo felt gratitude for this woman's company. They had little in common, yet Maggie's smile, framed by lines of age, was endearing.

Jo took a sip of her water, then set it down. "Tell me, what is it that you need courage for?"

Maggie took her own sip of wine.

Had her hands always trembled? Jo wondered. She supposed when someone reached their eighties and nineties that some trembling was expected.

Maggie picked up her fork again but didn't take a bite. "Did you know I grew up in California? Right in San Francisco."

Jo didn't, and she wondered where Maggie was going with this information.

"I was born in 1887," Maggie said. "To you, that probably sounds ancient."

"Not ancient . . ." Jo said, doing the math between 1887 and 1981. "You're ninety-four? That's impressive."

Maggie's smile was soft. "Except for my body slowing down, my mind doesn't know much difference between now and when I was nineteen."

Jo nodded and took another bite of her food, although Maggie had stopped eating for now. "I'm sure you've seen a lot of changes and advances in your day."

"Many, and not all for the better." Maggie's voice was quiet. "Do you remember learning about the great San Francisco earthquake of 1906?"

Jo blinked a couple of times. "Of course . . . were you there at the time?"

Maggie picked up her wine glass and took another swallow. "I was nineteen years old and on my way to my first day at the Pacific Dispensary for Women and Children when the earthquake hit. I was training to be a nurse, you see."

The hairs on Jo's arms stood up. "I didn't know you were a nurse."

"I was only in training for a short time," Maggie said. "After the earthquake and those terrible fires, I'd had enough of hospitals. I was a patient in one of them for three weeks because of my own injuries. Even now, I'll do almost anything to avoid stepping foot into a hospital ward."

Jo didn't know if her eyes could get any wider. She'd known nothing of this about Maggie, and she wondered what type of injuries the woman had from the earthquake. What little she'd shared so far had conjured up a dozen more questions. "What time did the earthquake hit?"

"Around five in the morning," Maggie said. "So many people lost their lives because they were in their beds. They couldn't get out of their apartments and homes fast enough. And then the fires—back then, most of the buildings were made of wood."

Jo shook her head. "I can't even imagine."

"No one could." Maggie looked down at her hands. "Until you're in the middle of it yourself, it's impossible to comprehend."

Jo's heart ached for the woman sitting across from her, and she rested her hand atop Maggie's. "How awful. What about the rest of your family?" Surely, she had parents, possibly siblings?

"All of them were killed." Maggie lifted her gaze. Her blue-green eyes were still beautiful even with tears in them.

Jo's throat squeezed.

"The events of that day, and the next few days, were surreal." Maggie moved her hand from Jo's and picked up her cloth napkin. After dabbing at her eyes, she said, "If it hadn't been for a young man named Orlando Gallo, I wouldn't be here today. I owe him my life."

Jo swallowed. "He helped rescue you?"

"More than that." Maggie folded her hands again. "He kept me alive until we could both be rescued. I guess you could say that he was the first man I . . . fell in love with."

Jo didn't know how this story could become more amazing and incredible, but every sentence was more astounding than the previous one. And who knew a ninety-four-year-old woman could still blush?

Maggie brought a hand to her flushed neck. "When we were rescued, he promised to find me after he was released from the hospital. But he never came." Her tears returned.

"I'm so sorry," Jo said. "Did you ever find out what happened to him?"

"No," Maggie said. "I never found out what happened to him, despite inquiries I've made over the years." She cleared her throat and met Jo's gaze head-on. "I was hoping that you could adjust your summer plans and take me to San Francisco for a few weeks. I have no children, no grandchildren, and I want to leave my estate to the descendants of the man who saved my life so long ago. In order to do that, I need to find out what happened to him."

Jo wasn't sure if she'd heard right. Maggie wanted her to go to San Francisco, and what? Dig through library archives? When she saw that Maggie's expression was perfectly in earnest, Jo felt irritated. First, she couldn't drop everything. And . . . she'd planned on working on her manuscript. *Really* working on it. Perhaps finishing it. And . . . *what?* Now wasn't the time to come to an epiphany that her summer plans were quite pitiful, yet aside from the manuscript-writing aspect, what did she have?

Maggie lifted a hand. "Don't answer yet. Come to my house, and I'll show you my scrapbook. If nothing else, you'll be humoring an old lady and her memories. But if you'd like to come with me on my investigative tour, then I'll make sure you're compensated for your time as a travel companion, and I can guarantee that we'll eat some of the best food ever created."

Chapter Four

San Francisco
April 17, 1906

"Coming, Ma!" Orlando Gallo called as he trod the stairs to the upper floor apartment he shared with his mother. She'd been watching from the window and had waved at him with some urgency.

Orlando couldn't guess what she wanted now, but everything with his mother was always urgent. Before his father died, Orlando supposed his father had been the one to curb Ma's fears, and Orlando had remained oblivious. Now, his mother stood in the open doorway of their apartment, refusing to take one step into the hallway, instead waiting for Orlando to come to her.

"Did you hear the news?" she asked, her round face flushed pink. Today had been hot for April, and Orlando had heard plenty of conversation and speculation about the beginning of a heatwave.

Orlando was tired enough from painting all morning by the wharf and trying to drum up new customers among the tourists and locals, and the heat hadn't helped. But he measured his words when he replied, "What news?"

"The plague is back." Ma's brown eyes were wide, and

there was a sheen of perspiration on her forehead. "I heard it when Mrs. Brooks talked to the newspaper boy."

"There's no plague." Orlando moved past her into their shared room. Someday, he planned to own an entire house. But right now, all they could afford was to rent a room from Mrs. Brooks. Orlando's mother hadn't learned much English yet, so she frequently misunderstood conversations she overheard.

"Look, Ma," he continued, holding up the paper sack he carried. In his other hand, he'd balanced his easel and box of paints. "I got that fried fish you like and some buns."

Food could always distract his mother, and she untied her apron. Why she wore an apron all day was a mystery to Orlando. She hadn't cooked since his father died, but she wore an apron until Orlando brought home dinner.

"Well, then, let's eat." His mother took her place at the small table in the corner of the room. Two chairs, a table, one mattress, a sleeping mat, and a washbasin were the only things in the sparse room. They'd hung a sheet from the ceiling to separate the single mattress from the rest of the room so that his mother had some privacy.

Orlando hid a sigh, wishing he wasn't the only son who'd remained in San Francisco with his mother. But as the baby of the family, when his mother refused to leave the city and seek their fortune elsewhere, Orlando had been the one left behind to care for her. He had two older brothers and three sisters. They'd all moved to other cities, finding occupations, marrying, and beginning their new lives in America. A letter from one of his siblings would be discussed for days by his mother.

If only Orlando could get a spot in an art gallery and gain recognition for his work.

"Wash your hands, son," his mother said.

"Ma, I told you that some paint doesn't come off with soap," he said. "It takes time." But he rose and crossed to the washbasin so that his mother would be satisfied with his efforts. He had to keep reminding himself that his mother's world was very small.

He returned to the table, and after his mother offered a blessing on the food, they began to eat. The food here was never as good as it had been in Italy, and although there were some restaurants around run by other Italians, it wasn't the same.

Orlando's father had told him that he should open a restaurant instead of drawing pictures that no one wanted to buy. Fortunately, Orlando's mother had been more supportive of his chosen profession. But when his father had died a couple of months after arriving in San Francisco, his mother had wanted to return to Italy. Luckily, his brothers had talked her out of that notion. Not only had their father sold their land and house, but his dream was for his children and grandchildren to have new opportunities in America.

His mother had lost the one person she was most dependent on, and without him, she refused to return to regular life. She wouldn't see any friends she'd made, and she spent her days pacing. As Orlando's siblings left one by one, he and his mom had to cut back on expenses. He didn't want to use up his father's estate money on renting. Besides, he'd only gotten a small share after the money was divided among his siblings. And he didn't want to spend his mother's money. What if something happened to him? What would she do?

"Aren't you hungry?" his mother asked.

Orlando couldn't remember a time in recent months when he *hadn't* been hungry. "Not too hungry." He slid the rest of his portion over to her. He'd get satisfaction from watching her eat her fill.

His mother used to be heavy-set, but she was about half her previous size now. And although her face was still round, Orlando hated seeing the changes of her weight loss and aging. It only reminded him of the passage of time, how he could never return to the happy memories of his childhood, and how much he missed his father.

Sometimes, Orlando wondered if he'd ever find a great love like his parents had. There were both good things and bad things about that type of marriage. Good because someone loved you deeply. Bad, because continued existence without the other was miserable.

"*Grazie*, Orlando," his mother said, drawing him from his thoughts. She'd finished eating.

He nodded and stood to clear the wrappers. It was nearly seven o'clock, and his mother would want to open the door so she could listen to any conversation Mrs. Brooks might have with the other boarders in the parlor downstairs. No matter what he said, or what Mrs. Brooks said, his mother wouldn't join the others. She'd content herself with sitting by the open doorway and listening from upstairs.

If only Orlando could get a spot in an art gallery and sell his larger paintings, he could move them from this small room. For even that expense, he didn't dare touch his mother's funds.

So, the days and nights passed much the same. Orlando spent his days hawking his art, and his mother paced a one-room flat, worrying about everything a person could possibly worry about.

His mother went to open the door and sit and listen, so Orlando knew he was free to work on the larger canvas painting he'd set up in the corner. At the wharf, he only painted small landscape scenes, still lifes, and whatever a passing patron might request. So he kept his larger canvases in the apartment. With the setting sun, he hoped that the temperature would cool, and he opened their single window to let in the night breeze. But no wind stirred, and Orlando removed his shirt so he could at least cool himself down a little. Then he stood in front of his easel and canvas and took stock of the work he'd done the night before.

He was painting a landscape of an Italian vineyard and a collection of rural homes. He hoped that someone from his homeland would be willing to purchase it for nostalgic purposes. And that same nostalgia would earn Orlando a decent wage.

His mother hadn't commented on it, which was unusual, but she would gaze at it several times a night. She rarely talked about their home in Italy anymore, and one part of Orlando was sad for that. It was like she'd given up on ever returning.

He didn't expect to return to Italy, either. He wanted to fulfill his father's dream, and when Orlando sat on the wharf each morning, watching the sun rise, it felt as if anything was possible. Hope renewed itself. But once he returned to the small apartment, the hope dimmed, and he had to brace himself to deal with his mother's anxieties and keep his wits about him until the next day.

Orlando painted until he heard his mother's soft snores coming from where she slept on the single mattress on the other side of the sheet. He stepped back from the canvas and surveyed his progress. Then he rolled his shoulders and rotated his neck, feeling the relief and ache in equal parts throughout his body. The painting would only take two or three more sessions, and then it would be finished. He'd let it dry for a full two weeks before hauling it to show some of the gallery owners.

He'd have to impress them with a larger painting because his smaller works hadn't caught their interest. Orlando knew he was tired, but he hadn't expected his eyes to burn as he followed the lines of his paint strokes—from the rolling green fields, to the sun-dappled trees, to the quaint farm homes.

Feeling homesick never did anyone any good, so Orlando cleaned his brushes, turned off the electric light, then settled onto his sleeping mat. The hardness had long since ceased to bother him. But no matter how exhausted he was, or how late he went to sleep, he always woke before dawn with the first birdsong.

April 18 was no different.

Orlando had become adept at moving silently about the apartment so that when he slipped out into the hallway, his mother still slept undisturbed. He crept down the stairs, mindful of the other renters, and purposely skipped the step that creaked. He was also careful not to let the paints and brushes in his portable box rattle, or to accidentally bump his easel against a wall or door frame.

Once outside, Orlando breathed in the morning air. No fog had settled the night before, so he was greeted with a clear, violet morning. His favorite time of day was the moment when the sun crested the eastern horizon, and its rays splashed a myriad of colors across the water. Golds, pinks, violets, and greens competed for attention in his artist's mind. And he painted them all, mixing paint colors, then mixing again, as he tried to capture the exact hues. He knew from experience that within thirty minutes of the sun's first appearance, the colors sharpened and spread, the pureness lost.

Only one other painter had arrived at the wharf as early as Orlando. They nodded to each other, but extended no other greetings since both wanted to focus on their craft. Orlando set up his easel and opened his box of paints and brushes. Within the hour, more artists would come and set up their easels, but Orlando relished the solitude. The sound of a rattling cart reached him, but Orlando didn't turn around. Eventually, the street behind him would become more populated with shop owners, newspaper boys, and cart merchants. Another artist showed up, and they greeted each other with a brief nod.

The scent of baking bread floated on the light breeze. The nearby bakery had opened. His stomach felt like a tight fist, but he usually skipped breakfast, so he was used to feeling the emptiness. By experience, he knew the sharp hollowness would soon ease. It was only when he started to feel light-headed that he knew he'd have to find sustenance.

A couple of men on bikes rode past, their work clothes telling Orlando they were on the way to a labor job. There was always something being built in the city. Orlando had even worked on some of the crews during the rainy months when painting at the wharf wasn't bringing in enough to buy fish for dinner.

Heels clicked on the cobblestone behind him, and Orlando turned to see a young lady walking with a brisk stride along the pedestrian walk. He guessed her to be nineteen or twenty, only a year or two younger than him. She wore a nurse's uniform, and her dark blonde hair was pulled back into a tight bun at the nape of her neck. The morning light reflected against the blonde, making her hair into a halo of gold. She was out early, but it made sense for a nurse who might work through the night. What caught his attention was her classic profile and graceful neck. He guessed her to be of Scandinavian descent, due to the creamy paleness of her skin tone.

She glanced over at him, and their gazes connected for a moment.

He couldn't look away from the blue-green of her eyes. She was, simply put, more lovely and brighter than the dawn.

It was the woman who finally broke their gaze. She lifted her chin and continued along the walkway. But Orlando had noticed a pink flush stain her neck before she averted her eyes. He smiled as he watched her move away, until a man with a cart blocked his view. Orlando blinked and returned to mixing colors. But all he saw was the woman—the proud lift of her chin, the graceful line of her neck, her womanly curves that dipped to a trim waist, the length of her legs . . .

He swirled his brush into a pale gray and outlined the woman's form on his canvas. Making swift, fluid strokes, he had her general shape down in seconds. He wanted to get as many details as he could before he forgot, although he didn't think he would forget. Using a darker gray, he made more definitive lines. Her calves, her shoulders, the swell of her hips.

Then his brush shifted, cutting a line right down the middle of the canvas. For an instant, Orlando wondered if he'd locked his knees, and one of them had buckled. Then the very earth beneath his feet moved with a shudder. The easel tipped and fell before he could grab it, but in the next moment, he realized it didn't matter. Because it sounded like a train was roaring beneath the earth, coming straight for him.

Orlando lost his balance, falling to his knees. Everything kept moving around him, and it seemed impossible to keep his balance. Someone was yelling or screaming, and the deep roaring continued. Across the street, the buildings were shaking, wood cracked, bricks fell, and Orlando caught sight of the nurse he'd noticed before. She was dodging falling bricks, and then he watched with horror as she fell, and the bricks continued to tumble on top of her.

He scrambled to his feet, his stomach roiling, and he ran toward the woman. He moved the bricks off her as fast as he could. She only stared at him as if she thought he was a ghost. Dust covered her face and clothing, and a cut on her temple was bleeding.

"You need to get out of the way," Orlando gasped. "The buildings are going to collapse."

The woman stared at him, saying nothing.

Orlando knew his English was decent, so the woman must be in shock.

More bricks fell around him, and Orlando didn't need to look up to know that they could both be buried if they didn't move. He scooped the woman into his arms; she didn't even protest. Other people were surging around him now, and he started to run, jostled by the crowd. He didn't know where they were going, but he had to get this woman to safety, then go find his mother.

Chapter Five

San Francisco
April 18, 1906

MAGGIE WONDERED IF SHE was in shock, or perhaps she was dreaming. Parts of her body felt numb, or maybe it was pain? It was hard to tell. But she did know a man was carrying her through the streets of San Francisco as screams echoed around them.

The aftershocks from the earthquake were fierce and terrible, and all Maggie could do was cling to this man's warm, strong neck and hope he wouldn't trip over the rubble and drop her. A selfish worry, she knew.

Her thoughts flitted to her family. Her sister and her parents. She'd left them sleeping in their modest home. Surely, the earthquake had awakened them, and Maggie could only pray they'd gotten to safety.

The young man was speaking to her, although his voice sounded strangely far away. "Do you remember your name?"

"Maggie," she said, her breath hitching. She gazed up at him. Seeing him, yet not comprehending fully how this was all happening. He was the man who'd been painting on the wharf. She'd noticed him right away—how could she not, with his striking looks? His eyes reminded her of the color of the wet earth in her mother's patio garden. His olive skin complemented his nearly black hair that waved against his shirt collar.

His gaze held hers for a moment before he said, "My name is Orlando. Do you remember how to count?"

She was about to say that, of course, she did, but then the earth wrenched again. Orlando stumbled, but somehow, he righted himself.

Maggie couldn't very well expect him to keep carrying her.

"I can walk," she said. "I need to get back. My sister and parents might be trapped."

"Are you sure?" he asked, his brows furrowing.

She was again captured by his eyes, which were so very dark. And he was younger than she'd first thought. Perhaps only a year or two older than she. His accent wasn't American, either. Before she could wonder more things about him, he said, "Here, I can support you if you're injured."

He lowered her to the ground, and she gingerly took a step. She ached all over, but she was still moving. After taking a steadying breath, she looked around at the demolition surrounding them. The road had buckled, and up ahead, there was a carriage tipped over. No one seemed to be doing anything about the stranded horses, though.

"We should help those horses," Maggie suggested.

Behind her, someone cried for help, and she turned to see Orlando crouch and extend a hand to a boy trying to climb out of a window with shattered glass.

He was about ten, and he had small cuts on his face.

Maggie moved toward the boy, wondering what she could do to help. Tears streaked his dusty cheeks, and his lower lip trembled as he tried to hold back cries.

"Are you all right?" Maggie asked. "Where are your parents?"

"I don't know," the boy cried, tears running down his cheeks. "The door is blocked, and I can't get out that way."

"It's all right, kid," Orlando said. "We'll help you out, then find your parents."

He sniffled and nodded.

Above them, something cracked, and Orlando called, "Watch out!" He yanked the boy out of the window and shoved him to the side.

She looked up as a portion of the roof from the building tumbled down, straight toward her. Orlando tugged her with him, trying to get out of the way, and in the process, he lost his balance. They both fell against the alley wall, but before either of them could get out of the way, debris rained down upon their heads.

Maggie covered her head with both arms, and she could only imagine what the others were experiencing. Orlando was closer to where the roof had been falling. And what about the young boy?

Another aftershock rumbled beneath her feet, and Maggie pressed herself against the vibrating wall, making herself as small as possible. As long as this wall held up . . . She'd hoped too soon, because a high-pitched whine sounded above her, and suddenly, the color of the sky disappeared.

Maggie drew into herself, covering her head again. Bricks tumbled down, hitting her shoulders, her back, and her arms as they fell. She cried out in pain, but there was nowhere to go, no way to escape.

Something heavy was on her legs. Part of the roof? No, it wasn't sharp or hard.

She heard breathing. *Orlando?* Everything else was black. Was the earth still trembling? Or was it her own body?

"Are you all right?" a male voice rasped.

Maggie swallowed against the dryness of her throat. "Orlando? Is that you?"

"Yes."

It was his body, then, that was half over hers. Protecting her from the worst of the falling roof. But what did that mean for Orlando? Yet, she was relieved. They'd been buried under rubble, it seemed, and she wasn't quite sure which way was up, but she wasn't alone.

Thank goodness.

"Where's the boy?" she asked.

"I shoved him out of the way," Orlando said in a low, muted tone. "But I was too late to spare you. I'm sorry."

A laugh bubbled up in her throat, but it refused to escape. Why was this man *apologizing*? For the earthquake? Ridiculous. "You probably saved my life more than once," she managed to say, even though she really needed something to soothe her aching throat. "I don't think you need to apologize."

Orlando didn't answer for a moment. His breathing was audible, though, fast and close. She guessed that his lower body was draped over hers, and his legs seemed to grow heavier by the minute. But it wasn't like she could tell him to move—what would happen to the rubble if he did?

Around them, the fallen roof and bricks seemed to have settled. There was no more crashing or tumbling. Yet, everything felt precariously balanced, even if Maggie couldn't see much. Or anything, more accurately.

Her eyes weren't adjusting, and the inky blackness began to feel suffocating.

"Do you still remember your name?" Orlando asked.

"Maggie." She paused, and despite the darkness and the fear rising inside of her, she said in a teasing tone, "Do you remember yours?"

His chuckle was soft. "Orlando."

Another aftershock had her grasping his shirt and burying her head against his shoulder.

"It's over," he said after a moment, and she lifted her head. There was nowhere to look, though, except into darkness.

The silence settled around them. "Why can't we hear anyone or anything?"

"People are moving as far away from the buildings as possible," Orlando said. "You shouldn't have followed me to that boy."

"What's done is done," Maggie said with a sigh. "He looked so terror-stricken. I hope he stays safe and can find his family soon."

"I hope so, too." He shifted beside her, but they both remained in the same position. "Am I hurting you?"

"I don't think so," she said truthfully. "I can't feel much, anyway."

"Let me try something." His shoulder lifted as he attempted to reach for something above them.

"Be careful," she said, but it was too late.

Bricks shifted around them, and the corner of one scraped her cheek.

Orlando released a groan. "I think my leg is broken."

"Oh, no." Maggie blinked back hot tears. Her mind raced through her nursing training, but they hadn't learned anything about broken bones yet or setting them. Did his leg need to be elevated? How much pain was Orlando feeling?

"Maybe I can move some of the bricks away—"

"No," he said. "It's too dangerous. More might cave in around us. Someone will come soon."

"We can't just wait, though." Prickles of heat skittered across her skin. This man was in pain, and what if he was bleeding? "I'm going to scream for help. You might want to cover your ears."

"Help!" she called loudly. Her next plea was even louder. "Help us! We're buried under the brick!"

Orlando soon added his calls to hers until they were both out of breath, and Maggie's throat felt like it had been scorched by hot sand.

"We should give it a break for a little while," Orlando said. "Wait until the aftershocks are finished and people are starting to clean up."

He was right, Maggie knew it, but that didn't stop the panic from thumping through her chest. She listened. For anything. Any sound from the outside.

But the quiet extended between them and beyond the rubble. It was an eerie sound. No streetcars. No wagons. No horse hooves. No voices. Only breathing and heartbeats could be heard.

"How soon?" she said after a moment, mostly to herself.

"The boy knows we're here," Orlando said. "He'll tell someone. There are probably bigger emergencies right now."

Maggie desperately wanted to believe him, so she did. She held onto his words with the passing moments. Soon, she noticed Orlando's breathing seemed off. Was he hyperventilating? Or maybe he had asthma? "What's wrong?" she asked. "Do you have asthma? I know something about that. I'm in nursing school—although we haven't dealt with broken bones yet, we have studied asthma."

"It's not asthma." His voice sounded older now, more tired. "It's the pain in my leg . . . or both legs, actually."

She drew in a breath before he said the next words.

"They're in bad shape," he said. "And the numbness is wearing off."

"I'm sorry . . ." Her voice choked with emotion.

"Don't apologize, remember?"

Maggie heard the bravery in his tone, but his labored breathing didn't lie. "I remember," she said, but new tears burned in her eyes. *She* was fine—bruised and scraped, yes, but fine for the most part. Yet, this young man had helped a complete stranger, and now he had broken legs.

She hated to think that he was suffering so much. Where were the people to rescue them? Had the little boy told anyone about the couple buried beneath a building of bricks?

Time crept by, and Maggie strained to listen for anyone coming near their spot. Another aftershock hit, and another. Not even Orlando could suppress his groans as the bricks shifted around them.

"I'm so sorry," Maggie whispered enough times that Orlando no longer told her not to apologize.

When the scent of smoke filtered through the bricks, Maggie hoped it was her imagination. "Do you smell that?"

"Yes," Orlando said.

"Something's on fire," Maggie said, wishing her voice wasn't laced with panic. "And it's close. What if . . ." She bit back a cry.

"Earthquakes create fires," Orlando said in a calm voice. "I'd be surprised if there wasn't a fire."

How could he be so calm?

"Put your head on my shoulder," he continued. "You'll be more comfortable."

"I don't want to cause you more pain, though," Maggie said.

She heard the smile in his voice when he next spoke. "I can think of worse things than sharing a small space with a beautiful woman."

If the circumstances had been different—much different—she might have blushed.

Maggie rested her cheek against his shoulder. Even though they were buried beneath bricks, she could still catch his scent. He smelled like the ocean, combined with oil paint, and a faint spice. It was comforting, somehow.

"Tell me about what you were painting," she said.

"On the wharf?"

"Yes."

"I paint whatever the tourists want me to."

Maggie was sure there was a story behind that, and she had more questions, but first, she asked, "What were you painting just before the earthquake?" *Just before I saw you? Just before our worlds shifted?*

"The sunrise."

Maggie closed her eyes even though that didn't change the darkness. She didn't always take time to admire the sunrise, but this morning, it had been beautiful.

"When did you first start painting?" she asked next.

"That's a long story."

"I have plenty of time."

She felt his laugh as his shoulder vibrated, and she found herself smiling in their confined space. He shifted his arm, and his hand brushed hers. When he linked their fingers, she was surprised. But not surprised enough to pull away. This was nice, she decided. And more comfortable, too. Which was probably why he'd shifted his arm, and they were now holding hands.

No matter.

He began his story, his voice a low timbre that was both soothing and made her feel like she could listen to him talk all day, and all night . . .

Chapter Six

Seattle
1981

JO TURNED THE NEXT page of the photo album, revealing another picture of the San Francisco earthquake destruction. She sat across from Maggie at her kitchen table. The hour was late, and they'd talked for hours, yet the story about Maggie and Orlando was fascinating.

"This was the corner of the building you were trapped under?" Jo asked, gazing at the pile of rubble. It was surprising that anyone could have survived being buried by so much brick.

"That's it," Maggie confirmed. "We were trapped for nearly twenty-four hours. It's amazing what you can learn about a person in such a time. You grow close emotionally. It might sound strange to fall in love in such a short period of time, but there it is. Yet I didn't know if I loved him because of our shared harrowing experience, so I wanted to find out. I wanted to spend more time with him."

She took another sip of her tea, and Jo noticed the trembling in her hands.

"I'm glad you had each other," Jo said. "I can't imagine what it would have been like if you'd been alone."

"I can't, either." Maggie looked down at her teacup. "Orlando Gallo was a godsend. I think we would have been great friends and our relationship would have progressed, if only..."

Her voice trailed off, and Jo didn't miss the emotion in it. "You had no way to contact him after."

"No." Maggie exhaled. "We were taken to different hospitals, you see. His legs had both been broken, and I knew he'd be laid up for a while. I inquired at every hospital and with every medical person I could find after my release." She shook her head slowly. "But the city was in chaos for so long. People had packed up what they could scrounge and moved across the bay or to other parts of California."

Jo turned the next page of the photo album. She pointed to a picture of the wharf and a man standing there, painting on a canvas. "Is this him? Did you find him?"

"No," Maggie said. "I took that picture to remind me of when I first saw Orlando. That wasn't him, though. I can't tell you how many times I walked that area over the next year, looking for him."

Jo was astounded. Maggie had spent a year looking for him. And even longer following the art circuit. "Yet you never saw any of his paintings?"

"Right. I could picture them in my mind, of course." Maggie's smile was soft, wistful. "He had a gift for description and storytelling."

Jo smiled in return. "And now you want to find out what happened to him, no matter the outcome?"

"I do," Maggie confirmed. "I know it's a long shot. Always has been. *I'm* ninety-four, so I don't expect to find him alive." Her voice faltered. "But I could find his children and give them the memories back. Not to mention my estate."

Out of all the details of the story Maggie had shared

tonight, this surprised Jo the most. Maggie was going to give all she had to veritable strangers. "You're a generous woman."

Maggie lifted a narrow shoulder. "I might change my mind. You know, if they're awful or something." The edge of her mouth lifted.

Jo released a soft laugh. "Right. That's a good plan." But *was* it? Was Maggie Howard a bit off her rocker with this idea?

"And that's where you come in, Jo," Maggie said, her eyes twinkling now. "No rush on the decision, but I would like to leave Friday, if at all possible. And you should know, Sadie is welcome to come. In fact, it would be a nice trip for her."

Jo wanted to laugh at the generous invitation to her dog, but having Sadie kenneled for a couple of weeks would be rough. Yet, Friday was in three days. She exhaled. Something was pushing her to say yes, and she didn't know why. It didn't make logical sense, but after hearing Maggie's story, Jo couldn't deny that she was also curious. She felt an impulse to say yes, but she also knew she should sleep on it.

"How about I let you know in the morning?" Jo said.

"Of course." The light in Maggie's eyes dimmed a bit, but her smile was bright.

It was after midnight when Jo returned home. She should have been exhausted, but instead, she spent the next hour digging through one of her encyclopedia sets to read more about the San Francisco earthquake. Sadie kept her company, her eyes half-closed.

"What do you think, girl?" Jo said, reaching over to scratch the dog's head. "Do you want to go on a road trip?" Sadie had been on plenty of shorter road trips in the past—mostly camping. Her disposition was mellow enough that she didn't cause much trouble beyond making sure she was fed and watered and had exercise breaks.

So it wasn't like Jo could use the dog as an excuse. Nor

her son. He'd be gone until mid-August. But what about her manuscript? Her writing style was to freehand, then type it up. If she had several chapters to type up when she returned home, that would be fine, right?

Jo laughed at herself. Was she really considering this madcap adventure with her ninety-four-year-old neighbor? Apparently, she was.

"All right, Sadie," Jo said into the dog's fur. "I'll call Liam in the morning, and if he's not opposed, then I'll go." It wasn't like she needed his permission—they were divorced, after all—but they still partnered in caring for their son.

And . . . Jo was still used to running things by Liam. She needed to detach from that. Break away and be her own person. It wasn't an overnight process, though. Not after being married for fourteen years.

Sadie closed her eyes, as if she thought it was a perfectly reasonable plan and it was now time to sleep on it.

"I agree," Jo said. "Let's go to bed."

That got Sadie's attention, and she lumbered to her feet. Jo turned out lights as she headed up the stairs, the dog padding after her. When Liam had moved out, Jo had stuck with her resolve that there be no pets in the bedrooms. But little by little, she began to make exceptions, and Sadie went to sleep at the foot of Alec's bed. By the time Jo woke up in the morning, Sadie would be at the foot of her bed.

Jo changed into her favorite leggings and oversized hoodie, then remembered that Liam wasn't here to keep the house at subpar temperatures. So she stripped off the hoodie and climbed into bed. Sadie took her spot at the foot of the bed—on Liam's side. Yes, Jo still slept on "her" side after all this time.

Closing her eyes, she thought of a young Maggie, and what the 1906 earthquake must have been like. Jo also wondered about Orlando Gallo. She couldn't help it. She was hooked on the story. What *had* happened to him? Her imagination turned out one possibility after another.

Had he arrived at Maggie's hospital room just moments after she'd left? Had he tried to find her, but in a series of mishaps, they kept missing each other time and time again? The thoughts were torturous, and they were only a fraction of what Maggie must have experienced over years of not knowing.

Had Orlando been struck down with another illness? Maybe a fever? Had he made it out of the hospital alive? Maybe he'd returned to his home country of Italy? Or had he moved across the bay and found a new love?

It was quite remarkable to think of how the pair had fallen in love . . . Well, Maggie had fallen in love with him. But Jo liked imagining that the event was mutual.

Somehow, sleep came, and when Jo awakened, she immediately thought of the road trip.

She really was excited, she realized. But first things first. She made coffee, with Sadie chomping on her food a few feet away. Then she took the mug of coffee into the shared office that had mostly been used by Liam. Jo opened the second drawer of the filing cabinet and pulled out two binders. One with her finished chapters, and the other with research notes.

She skimmed her notes on Genghis Khan and how he'd raised the status of women, giving his daughters and consorts positions of power. These women, or "Mongol queens", played vital roles in diplomacy and warfare. Of course, that all came crashing down when Khan died, and his successor, Ögedei, purged all his female relatives.

What was two weeks in the scheme of things? Or even three? She could review the research on their downtimes, and write at least a few more chapters from the point she'd gotten to. And she might even be able to do more research in San Francisco if they ended up at libraries.

Jo glanced at the clock. It was much too early to call her son on a summer day, but not too early to call Liam. He'd always been the early riser in their family. The one who made the coffee. The one who took Sadie on her morning walk.

Jo pushed back the nostalgia that contrasted sharply with the betrayal in her heart. She reached for the phone and called her ex-husband's number.

He answered on the third ring, and the gruffness of his voice made it clear that she'd awakened him.

"Oh, I didn't think you'd still be sleeping." Who was Jo kidding? Liam was no longer her husband, and his patterns could have very well changed with his new fiancée and new house.

"Jo?" Liam said, the raspy tone clearing a little. But it was still his tired voice, a sound that Jo had once found sexy. She pressed two fingers against her temple.

"Yeah, uh, hi," she said. "Sorry to call so early."

"Is this about Alec?" he asked. Someone murmured in the background. A woman's voice. *His fiancée.*

Heat crawled up Jo's neck. "No. Um. Well, not exactly. I mean, I wanted to tell you that I'm going to San Francisco with our—my—neighbor. Maggie Howard. Do you remember her?"

"Sorry, it will be a second," Liam whispered—*to his fiancée.*

Shuffling sounded, then a door clicked closed.

"What was that?" Liam asked, louder and more clear now.

Jo's pulse thudded at the base of her neck as she repeated herself.

"All right," Liam said. "Call with your hotel number when you get there in case Alec wants to talk."

"Yes, of course," Jo said. "But we're driving, so it will probably be better if I call him. I'll check in often, though."

The silence on the other end was so long that Jo wondered if they'd been disconnected. "Liam?"

"Did you say you're *driving*?"

"Yes."

"Why would you drive that far when you're the only one who can drive? We both know Mrs. Howard lost her license years ago. And we both know that you're distracted at best when driving."

An edge touched his voice. Why did that bother her, and why did she care? It wasn't like she needed his approval. So maybe she always needed detailed directions when she was driving, but it wasn't due to distractions. This was an old, tired argument between them. "Well, we're not in a hurry, and as long as we're heading south, we'll get there."

At one point in their relationship, Liam might have laughed. But that was before... *before* all the stuff...

"You should fly," Liam said. "Then you won't be liable. She's what? Ninety?"

"Ninety-four," Jo answered. The heat in her neck had spread to her chest, churning until it became indignation. "This is not up for debate. I'm letting you know that starting Friday, I'll be on the road, and you won't be able to call me if Alec needs something."

The silence was a stunned one this time.

Jo was both proud of herself, and a tiny bit horrified. She should be able to put her foot down with a man who'd shattered her heart into a million pieces.

"Jo, be reasonable." Liam's voice was louder now, and surely, his fiancée could hear every word.

"Tell Alec I'll call him this afternoon," Jo rushed to say because she felt the tears building. How was she having any of this conversation with the man she thought she'd spend the rest of her life with? The man who used to bring her flowers? The man who danced with her in the kitchen on rainy days?

Did he do those things with his fiancée?

Too late. Tears were already burning, and so she took a deep breath and hung up the phone. Then waited for it to ring with Liam calling back. One minute passed. Two. He didn't call.

Well, then, that was that.

Sadie nudged her leg, and Jo absently stroked the dog's head. "What do you think, girl? Want to road trip to San Francisco?"

Sadie's ears perked up.

"Then that's what we'll do."

Chapter Seven

MAGGIE BRUSHED HER SKIRT over her knees as they neared the final stop of the day. They'd grab a bite of dinner at a place that she'd planned in advance, then check into a motel in Medford, Oregon. If Jo was bothered by the extremely detailed schedule, she hadn't said anything. As it was, Jo had seemed lost in her thoughts most of the day.

Maggie couldn't guess at what her neighbor was thinking, but she was grateful that she'd decided to come along. Sadie hadn't been one spot of trouble. The dog currently sat in the back with her eyes glued to the passing scenery. She'd already taken one nap that morning.

Now, Maggie turned down the radio, set to a classical station that went in and out depending on where they were driving. It had provided a nice calm when their conversation of the morning had faded away. Maggie had learned some interesting things about her neighbor, primarily that she was a woman who never took time for herself.

And Maggie had just cut into that potential—at least for the next week or two. She'd also been fascinated to learn that Jo was working on a book as well.

"Turn on this street," Maggie instructed as Jo slowed down for a stop sign. The maps that Maggie had purchased for the trip were labeled and numbered so the transition from city to city and state to state would be smooth.

"Looks homey," Jo commented as they turned into the parking lot of the restaurant.

"I hope you don't mind Italian again," Maggie said. The restaurant was dark brick, with cheerful planters in two windows on either side of the blue-painted door.

"I don't mind." Jo's smile was faint, as if her thoughts were still far away.

"Why don't you have Sadie stretch her legs before we go inside," Maggie offered.

"All right." Jo climbed out, and her clothing tugged in the wind. She opened the back door, and Sadie barreled out, knowing the drill by now.

While Jo was taking care of the dog, Maggie pulled down the visor and checked her reflection in the mirror.

She adjusted the collar of her blouse, then added a pinch of color to her cheeks from the compact in her purse. By the time she was ready, Jo was back with Sadie. They cracked the windows, and Sadie climbed in the back of the car.

"We'll bring you a good treat, girl," Jo crooned.

Maggie smiled at the endearment. She and her husband had never had pets, not even a fish. Too much traveling, she supposed. Speaking of traveling . . . they were less than a day away from San Francisco now, and Maggie wondered if all of her plans would work out.

The Italian restaurant was small and quaint, which was how Maggie liked them. She was a bit stiff from being in the car for so long, so the restaurant was a nice change of pace. A young man approached them, wearing a white shirt and black vest. She guessed him to be around thirty, and a quick glance at his hand told her he wasn't wearing a wedding ring. Hmm . . . Maggie certainly appreciated his classic good looks, deep-set brown eyes, wavy black hair, and golden olive skin.

But Jo barely looked at him.

After they ordered, and the waiter had walked away, Maggie said, "He was a handsome fellow."

Jo's eyes snapped to Maggie's. "Who? The waiter?"

Maggie folded her hand on top of the table. "Yes, the waiter. He seemed to be friendly toward you."

"Mrs. Howard—"

"Maggie, remember?"

Jo cleared her throat. Was she blushing? "Maggie, I . . . uh . . . I'm not in the market for dating." She leaned closer. "Besides, we're in Medford. It's a long way from Seattle."

Maggie pursed her lips for a moment. "If it's right, it's right. Believe me, I have enough regrets to last two lifetimes."

At this, Jo's brows furrowed, a small V forming between them. "I'm sorry for the loss of Orlando when you had such hopes. But Liam *was* my Orlando. At least I thought so in our early marriage." She looked down at the table and shifted her utensils around.

"I don't mean to pry, but have you dated at all, since . . ."

Jo met her gaze. "I was set up once, but he had to cancel, and we never ended up going out. I just . . ." She inhaled as if she was thinking of something she regretted. "It's just hard. To move on. You know?"

Maggie nodded. If anyone understood, it was her.

Jo continued shifting her utensils about. "Alec is more and more like his father every week, and that only makes the pain more raw, I guess."

Maggie reached over and placed a hand over Jo's. "These things take time."

"I know," Jo said in a quiet voice. "But Liam is engaged again. He's completely moved on from me. Started a new life. Some days, it hurts more than others."

"Like today?" Maggie prompted. "You've been so quiet."

Jo bit her lip. "I'm sorry. I want to be a fun road trip partner."

With a shrug, Maggie lifted her hand. "I'm not worried. We have plenty of time, and I'm so used to being by myself that any type of company is great."

Jo's cheeks tinged pink. "You're sweet. But I promise I'll be more engaging. In fact, I'd love to hear about our scheduled stops tomorrow."

This made Maggie all kinds of pleased. "Well, I have my daily planner right here."

"Of course, you do," Jo said with a laugh.

It was good to hear the woman laugh, so Maggie offered a generous smile and pulled out the black and pink planner she'd made careful notes in. She wasn't surprised when Jo's eyes widened at the color-coded schedule inside the planner.

"That's very . . . detailed," Jo said at last after she had a chance to read over a couple of things. "You are a traveling guru."

Maggie only nodded.

"We have a meeting soon after we arrive tomorrow night?"

"Yes, with a museum director," Maggie said. "And . . ." She tapped the page on the morning block of the following day. "We'll be meeting with the director of one of the libraries as well. We might as well get advice from the woman who will know where to direct us best."

"You've done so much legwork already," Jo said, awe in her tone. "If Orlando can be found, then we'll definitely find him."

Maggie didn't let the vote of confidence go to her head. She very well knew that she had a very slim chance of finding a ninety-six-year-old Orlando Gallo alive and well.

The waiter walked up to their table carrying steaming plates of pasta, garlic bread, and a selection of delectable sauces. Once he left, with a smile to both ladies, Maggie said, "If you don't want his phone number, then I'll have you know that the museum director has a very nice voice. Sounds young, too. Not too young, of course. But definitely single."

Jo had just taken a sip of her drink and nearly spat it out in laughter. "How does one *sound* single?"

Maggie winked. "You'll see."

Jo merely shook her head. "I hope you didn't bring me on this road trip to try to set me up with random waiters or museum curators."

"Never," Maggie said. "But you must know that you're a lovely woman and you shouldn't give up hope of love."

Jo's eyes fell at that. "I haven't given up hope, exactly. I've written it off."

The waiter returned to refill their glasses, and after he left, Maggie wriggled her eyebrows. "I can ask him for his number if you're too shy."

"No," Jo said. "He's handsome, and I'm sure a perfectly decent guy, but he's not my type."

This caught Maggie's attention. "Oh, and what's your type, dear?"

Jo looked like she regretted saying a thing, but she was a good sport after all. "I guess the type I married. The scholarly professor type. Although, I'd prefer him to not have a straying heart."

"That's a step in the right direction," Maggie said. "Knowing your type. What you do and do not like."

Jo gave a brief shrug. "Like I said, I'm not interested in dating. Maybe someday."

Maggie hummed an *all right* because while she fully believed Jo, there was a bit of spark coming back into her eyes as they'd been chatting. If there was one thing Maggie believed, it was to never give up. Being alone as she was, she'd found she quite enjoyed her own company. But it also left a lot of time for dwelling on what might have been . . . what could have been.

After their meal, and after Jo had stayed quiet when Maggie had chatted with the waiter a few extra minutes, the two women and the dog checked into their motel.

Maggie was looking forward to a good night's rest, but she wanted to be on the road again at the crack of dawn. "Is six a.m. all right?" she asked Jo.

"Sure," Jo said without hesitation. If she'd been surprised, she didn't show it.

"Good night, dear," Maggie said.

"Thank you. For everything." Jo gave a sheepish smile. "It was fun tonight. And I'm already starting to unwind on this trip. I guess I didn't realize how much I've kept things buried deep."

Maggie squeezed the younger woman's hand. *She* should be the one thanking Jo.

Before Maggie turned in for the night, she withdrew an old journal from her luggage. The leather was cracked, and the pages had yellowed with time. She flipped to the final page and began to write.

Dear Orlando,

I have neglected this journal for years. I wrote in it for months after the earthquake, and then only sporadically after that. Once, Bruce found this journal and laughed because he thought I'd named it Orlando. Well, I suppose I have. But I didn't write again during our marriage.

I suppose it was because I thought that if I had moved on, then perhaps you have, too. At least, I hope you have. I hope you've had a wonderful life, a fulfilling life. And if I do find you, all the better, or if I find your children or grandchildren, it will be an honor to meet them.

For, you see, I'm heading to San Francisco again. To look for you.

Chapter Eight

Jo held back a laugh as the museum director introduced himself. He was in his fifties, and yes, his voice did sound younger. The ring on his left ring finger shouted loud and clear that he was a married man. She knew Maggie had noticed it, and Jo would make every effort to razz her about it later.

"Thank you for taking this appointment, Mr. Greenwood," Maggie said. "We know it's on a day you're closed, but we have a lot of ground to cover."

"Of course." Mr. Greenwood adjusted his horn-rimmed glasses. "Follow me."

Jo walked with Maggie along the corridor. Maggie latched onto Jo's arm—something she'd been doing that day, and Jo wondered if maybe this trip had been too much for the elderly woman after all. But Maggie kept insisting that she was fine—just achy from two days in the car.

Well, Jo was, too.

Still.

Maggie had been magic, though, in finding a rental house that allowed dogs. Sadie was perfectly content in the fenced-in backyard, and so at least Jo could relax about that. She'd also talked to her son this morning. He'd been in a rush to go on a hike with his dad and future stepmom, so the conversation only lasted a handful of minutes.

Jo had tried not to feel let down. She was on her own adventure, after all. But that wasn't it. Until the divorce, Jo had been the one to pack the lunches and organize hiking gear for their family hikes. Now . . . it was someone else.

"We'll start in here." Mr. Greenwood stopped in front of a door labeled *Private, Room 8*. "This is our archives specific to the 1906 San Francisco Earthquake. If there's anything in the museum about the man you're seeking, it will be in here." He swung open the door and flipped the light switch.

Fluorescent lights buzzed, flickering, then growing stronger. The long, narrow room was neatly organized, but Jo could practically taste the dust on her tongue. A small table with a microfiche machine sat in the middle of the room. And against the walls were shelves stacked with microfilm containers.

"Goodness," Maggie said, echoing Jo's exact thoughts. "Wherever shall we begin?"

At this, Mr. Greenwood scratched his temple. "They're organized by subject, or topic, if you will. Things should be fairly accurate, though errors are possible."

Jo nodded, but Maggie's eyes were comically rounded.

"Can you show us how to work the microfilm machine?" Jo asked. Might as well dive right in, although there was no way they'd be able to get through all the microfilm in this room. That would take a single person months.

"Sure thing." Mr. Greenwood gave a quick demonstration of the machine, which wasn't too complicated. By the time he finished, Jo realized that Maggie hadn't even been listening, but stood perusing the shelves.

"Well, thank you," Jo said. "When we leave, what's the best exit?"

The Healing Summer

Mr. Greenwood hesitated. "The same way you came in. The doors will automatically lock behind you."

"Very good," Jo said. With the man gone, she turned to Maggie. "Well, which should we take down first?"

Maggie turned to Jo. "I don't know about this," she said in a dejected tone. "There's just so . . . much. I think I've made a mistake."

Jo released a breath. "We already planned on being in San Francisco for two weeks. So, let's work on these today, and see what it brings us. We can't give up before we've truly started."

"You're right." Maggie blinked rapidly. "It's sounded like a good idea all along, but now that we're here, I'm second-guessing myself."

Jo stepped back from the microfilm machine. "Why don't you sit here, and I'll start pulling potential research."

Maggie seemed mollified at that and took a seat.

Jo began scanning titles and paused on one that said something about firefighters. "Didn't you say that firefighters were the ones to dig you out?"

"Yes," Maggie said.

Jo set the reel box on the table and helped Maggie load it. While she slowly looked through the articles and images, Jo moved to the next shelf. She scanned the titles, then stopped on one that referenced hospitals. She picked up the reel box and set it on the table as well. Over the next fifteen minutes, she had collected eight different boxes.

When she pulled up a chair next to Maggie, they took turns reading aloud headlines, then scanning through the articles.

Maggie was much better at deciphering the pictures than Jo was since she was familiar with the street names and neighborhoods of San Francisco.

They went through hospital records, but nowhere was the name of Orlando Gallo. Or even Gallo.

"It's like he disappeared," Maggie said. "Completely."

Jo sat back in her chair. A couple of hours had passed, and she was due for a break. "Do you think he gave a false name?"

Maggie frowned. "Why would he do that?"

"Insurance? Never mind. It was just a thought."

Maggie released a sigh. "If he did, then all of this will be fruitless, but I can't imagine him doing so."

"What about..." It was a bizarre idea, but maybe it would help. "What if he didn't go to a hospital, but some other place. Like a clinic? Or a rescue center."

"Rescue center?"

"Oh, when I was in college, I took a class on women's suffrage," Jo said. "There were mission homes in major cities that offered refugees a safe haven. They were funded by various churches, and they had education courses and provided medical services as well."

Maggie was silent for several minutes. "He was Catholic. Were there Catholic ones?"

"Maybe, but I don't think they checked your religion," Jo said.

Maggie's smile was brief. "You're probably right. So, now what?"

"We call them and ask them to check their archives, or we offer to do it ourselves."

So, twenty minutes later, they let themselves out of the building into the mild summer evening. "How about Mr. Greenwood?" Jo said as she opened the passenger door for Maggie. "Single, didn't you say?"

"I'm not always right," Maggie quipped, her eyes flashing with humor. "Just most of the time."

Jo laughed. "I'll let this one go, only because this trip is all about Orlando."

Maggie gave a dainty shrug before she climbed into her seat.

Once Jo had the car started, she backed out of their parking spot and headed toward their rental house. As she drove, they passed a corner with a phone booth. A man was inside, animatedly speaking to someone.

"I'm assuming you looked up all the Orlando Gallos in the San Francisco phone book and called them?" Jo said.

"Of course," Maggie said. "I did it again about five years ago. I found nine men of the same name. Nothing panned out."

"What about the surrounding cities?"

"Those, too. Twenty-eight dead ends."

Jo fell silent, thinking. Perhaps the mission homes would be the lead they were looking for. Or their library excursion tomorrow would bring new ideas as well. "What about calling all of the names with the last name Gallo?"

Maggie puffed out a breath of air. "That would take days of nonstop calling," she said.

"We have days." Jo glanced at her. "And you have *me* to help now."

Maggie's mouth curved. "Very true."

Jo started the moment they got to the rental. Well, after she played with Sadie, helped Maggie fix a meal from the groceries they'd bought, and spoke to Alec for a few moments. Jo created a paper trail system organized by city. Then she started calling the Gallo names in the phone book in the house. Tomorrow, they could make copies of the Gallo names from the phone books in the library.

It was an interesting experience calling strangers, but the more Jo did it, the more savvy she became. At least, in her own opinion. The work was exhausting, and even Maggie seemed worn out after Jo had called nearly twenty families. Two hadn't answered at all. But the ones who had denied knowing an Orlando Gallo who'd been born in the 1880s. A few times, though, Jo wondered if she was speaking to a person who was knowledgeable, or if they were just trying to politely get her off the phone.

When it neared nine p.m., she knew she had to quit for the day.

Sadie had fallen asleep at her feet, and Maggie looked like she was ready to drop into bed.

"We'll try the rest of the numbers in the morning," Jo said.

"Thank you," Maggie said. "It might all be a waste of time." Her tone was dejected again, as it had been at the microfilm room.

Jo hadn't expected Maggie's spirits to dampen. She'd been so enthusiastic and confident.

Maggie went off to bed, and Jo reviewed her list again. Maybe she should call a few more people, to cross them off. She glanced at the ticking clock over the tidy kitchen—9:10 p.m. She dialed.

The woman who answered sounded like she was in her sixties, perhaps.

"Hello, this is Jo Sampson, and I'm trying to track down a former acquaintance for my grandmother." It sounded better saying "grandmother" versus "elderly neighbor in Seattle." She continued before the woman could say anything else. "His name is Orlando Gallo, and he lived in San Francisco in the early 1900s."

"What did you say?"

"Orlando Gallo? San Francisco?"

"What's your name?"

"I'm Jo Sampson."

"And where are you from?"

Jo was fine with being patient, but this woman was an interrogator. "Seattle, actually, as well as my grandmother. She lived in San Francisco right before the 1906 earthquake, and—"

"Are you trying to sell me earthquake insurance?"

"No, ma'am," Jo said, keeping her tone calm. "I'm looking for an old friend of my grand—"

"What company are you with?"

"I'm not with a company," Jo said. "I'm a professor in Seattle, but that's not—"

"What's your phone number?" the woman cut in.

Jo wanted to laugh, or hang up, or both. Instead, she said, "I'm renting a place in San Francisco, and the number here is . . ."

Once she'd given the number, the woman said, "I already have insurance."

"I understand," Jo said. "I'm not calling about that—"

The line went dead. Jo set the receiver down, disbelief coursing through her. Well, now an older lady had the rental house phone number. Where was the harm in that? Maybe it was time to call it a night. Start tomorrow fresh.

Chapter Nine

MAGGIE EXTENDED HER HAND to Ms. Wu, the library director, and the two women shook hands. They'd spoken over the phone more than once, and the woman was even nicer in person. Her petite frame was dressed neatly in a pale blue blouse and black slacks, and her dark hair was a smooth bob, accented by a blue headband. Maggie guessed the woman to be in her early thirties.

"Come this way," Ms. Wu said. "And please call me Allison."

The library smelled of books and leather, and Maggie loved it. She glanced over at Jo, who was preoccupied with scanning the tall bookcases and the unique layout of the library. On the drive over this morning, they'd both discussed their mutual love for reading. So Maggie smiled at the look of awe on Jo's face. She felt the same way.

Allison led them into an office of sorts that looked like it needed some TLC. Books and stacks of paper covered every surface, from the two desks in the room to a cabinet and a bookcase.

To her credit, Allison didn't acknowledge or apologize for the disarray. Instead, she motioned for them to take seats and then sat across from them at the larger desk. "I asked one of our interns to compile a list of sources—articles and books—that might help you." She handed over a stapled group of papers. "We don't have all of these references at our library, but in the margin, she marked which libraries you can find them at. Now, one option would be to have the books sent to your local library in Seattle on an interlibrary loan."

Maggie glanced down at the list of books and articles. Right off, she could see there were a few she'd already been through. But the list would still be a huge help. "This is amazing. Thank you so much."

Allison folded her hands atop the desk. "I'll admit, I'm quite caught up in your adventure, too. When you told me about Orlando Gallo over the phone, I got curious." She picked up a thin red book on the desk and opened it. Then she tapped one of the pages with a finger. "This is a log of passengers who took the ferry across the bay a few days after the earthquake. If your Orlando wasn't too injured, perhaps he was on one of these ferries? Or perhaps a family member took him to another hospital in another city?"

Maggie tilted her head. She hadn't thought of this. "May I?"

"Now, I haven't found his name." Allison handed over the red book. "But that doesn't mean he didn't end up in another city. Of course, you mentioned you've called all the Orlando Gallos in surrounding cities."

"I have," Maggie said. "But now Jo is expanding that to all of the Gallo names. She started calling yesterday. In fact, we'd like access to any phone books you have here."

Allison's brows lifted. "Certainly." She looked at Jo. "Any luck yet?"

"Nothing yet," Jo said. "Most people think I'm a saleswoman."

Allison's right cheek dimpled. "Hopefully, you'll find a

lead." Her gaze shifted back to Maggie. "Have you thought about putting a notice in the newspapers?"

Maggie stilled at this. "What would I say?"

"That you're seeking information on a particular Orlando Gallo, and maybe offer a monetary award? Or maybe not."

Maggie considered this. "We might get to that point." She held up the list of references. "This will be very helpful, though."

With a nod, Allison said, "I'll have those copied phone book pages at the front desk for you soon. And you're welcome to use this office or any other part of the library."

"Thank you, Allison," Maggie said.

"Yes, thank you," Jo added with a smile.

Once they were alone in the cramped office, Jo said, "Well, should I locate the sources, and you start reading through them?"

Maggie was once again grateful for her neighbor's help. "That sounds wonderful." Today was a better day, she decided. She wasn't as exhausted and being in San Francisco made her feel closer to Orlando and their shared experiences.

She leafed through the red book with the ferry logs as she waited for Jo to return.

"Here we are," Jo said, walking back into the office with three books and several magazines. "How many of these have you looked through before?"

Maggie examined the materials. "I don't think I've seen any of them. Maybe the books are more recent publications." It had been a long time since 1906, after all.

Jo settled into one of the chairs, picked up a book, and began to scan through it.

About two hours into their research, Maggie was fighting to stay alert. At home, she took a small nap most days, but it wasn't even lunchtime yet. Somehow, Jo seemed in tune and said, "I think we need a break. Let's go on a walk and find a sandwich shop or something."

"That is going off our schedule," Maggie said with a teasing smile.

Jo smiled back. "I think we've earned it."

"I agree."

"First, let me check in with Alec, then we'll head out."

Maggie nodded and began to stack the magazines they'd already browsed. She couldn't help hearing Jo's conversation over the phone—after all, they were in the same room.

"Hi . . . Liam. Is Alec around?"

A pause.

"Oh. That's nice," Jo said, her tone sounding falsely bright. "I'm sure he's loving that. When do you think they'll be back?"

Another pause.

"All right. Great." She closed her eyes. "I'll call back later on, then."

Liam must have said something else because Jo said, "Working hard." She opened her eyes and glanced at Maggie. "We're at the library right now going through several sources . . . No . . . Maggie is great. She runs circles around me, not the other way around."

Maggie decided that Jo was feeling decidedly uncomfortable with her ex-husband's line of questioning.

"I should go, Liam," Jo said. "Nice to hear your voice." She hung up and groaned.

"Is everything all right?"

Jo perched on the edge of the desk, and miraculously, none of the clutter fell off. "First of all, I told him it was nice to hear his voice." She exhaled. "I'm pathetic, that's what. Is it still possible to be in love with a cheating ex-husband who's engaged to another woman?"

Maggie rose slowly to her feet, using the edge of the desk for support. It always took her a moment to adjust from sitting to standing. She moved closer to Jo and rested a hand on her shoulder. "Don't be so hard on yourself. Love doesn't just vanish into thin air. Maybe you'll always love him, in a way."

Jo released a breath. "Yeah . . . And to make it worse, *my* son is with *his* fiancée at some arcade place for a birthday party for one of the other kids in the neighborhood. He's only been there a few days, and he already has friends. Which is great. But *I'm* the one who should be taking him to his friends' birthday parties." She wiped at her budding tears. "I think I'm ordering dessert after lunch. Something with chocolate."

"That's what I like to hear. Let's go, partner."

The two women left the library and walked along the city sidewalks until they found a bakery tucked between a Chinese restaurant and a laundry business. The bakery served soup, sandwiches, and pastries. Maggie had to laugh when Jo picked out two brownies, then promptly ate one before starting on her chicken salad sandwich.

"Better?" Maggie teased.

Jo offered a sheepish smile. "Actually, yes. I mean, I still have all my problems, but double-fudge brownies help."

"I'll try mine after lunch," Maggie said.

"Oh, these are both mine."

The women laughed. Maggie was happy to see the warmth back in Jo's brown eyes. She was too young, too accomplished, too full of life to be pining after a man who was living a new one. Yet Maggie knew she wasn't one to talk—how long had she been pining for Orlando? Logically, she'd moved on with her life, and had even put her whole heart into her marriage. But there had always been that one part of her, sometimes buried, sometimes surfacing, that had never forgotten the young man who'd kept her sane and safe in the darkest time of her life.

"How about we be tourists for a few hours?" Maggie said. "I'd like to show you in person where Orlando painted on the wharf and the corner where we were trapped. But we can sightsee on the way there."

"I'd love that," Jo said.

Once they'd finished eating, Maggie directed Jo as they drove toward the San Francisco Bay. The summer weather sparkled with heat, but Maggie didn't mind. She found an oldies station on the radio, and when an Elvis Presley song came on, Jo sang along to the words.

"I'm impressed," Maggie said as the song drew to a close.

"My grandmother played Elvis nonstop at her house," Jo said. "It used to drive me crazy, but now the music brings in memories that I'm happy to remember." She turned onto Hyde Street and found a parking place in front of an apartment building.

"This is perfect," Maggie said, waiting for the car to be in park before she climbed out.

Jo was there to help her within seconds, which Maggie appreciated. Over the last couple of years, she'd swallowed any misguided pride and accepted any offers of help.

They walked beneath the shade of the trees until they reached the traffic light on the corner. Once it was green, they headed across the street, toward the wharf. Already, the salty sea breeze and the call of the circling seagulls were bringing back the memories in a rush.

Artists were stationed haphazardly about, some painting, others with small carts holding their creations to sell to tourists. But Maggie bypassed them all, not interested in their modern offerings, but wanting to remember the past.

She finally stopped in a space a few yards from a docked boat. "This was where he had an easel set up," she told Jo. "I was heading that way, and our gazes connected for a moment."

Maggie let go of Jo's arm and folded hers against the breeze. It wasn't cold, not really, but she wanted to keep her reminiscing close. "He was striking. Dark-haired, dark eyes, but full of life and warmth, and intellect. And his skin was as golden as the dawn. I was relatively shy, and I looked away quickly. But before I completely passed by, I glanced over again."

Jo smiled as she listened.

"He was watching me," Maggie said. "A half-smile on his face. It wasn't like I thought he'd approach me or catcall—no, nothing like that. It was friendly, that's all. He gave a small nod, or at least I thought he did, and that's when the earthquake hit."

"Wow," Jo breathed. "So many lives changed in an instant."

Maggie nodded, blinking against the breeze. Her eyes had started to water, and she blamed it on the salty air. "Sometimes, you have a feeling about a person. You don't even have to know them or speak to them, but you can tell they are a good soul."

"Yes," Jo said.

"That was Orlando Gallo," Maggie said. "I can't think of a better person to be buried alive with." She chuckled at her own words. "Sorry, that sounds morbid, I suppose. But it's true."

"I believe it." Jo set her arm about Maggie's shoulders. "Between you and me, and a few prayers, I think we'll get lucky this week."

Maggie leaned against the much sturdier Jo. "I hope so. If not—"

"We're not to the *if not* stage yet," Jo said in a determined tone. "We still have a lot of phone calls to make and references to read through."

Maggie nodded but remained quiet as her memories filtered through her mind. *Where are you, Orlando? What happened to you?*

Chapter Ten

SAN FRANCISCO WAS BEAUTIFUL, but Jo wasn't able to appreciate it as much as she wanted to. Her eyes were blurry, and her brain foggy with exhaustion from more hours spent at the library. She could only imagine how Maggie felt. The woman had headed to bed soon after their shared dinner. So Jo walked onto the back deck, where she could make phone calls and hang out with Sadie while at the same time keeping things quiet so Maggie could sleep.

"How was your day, girl?" she asked Sadie.

The dog's chin rested on Jo's knee, and she looked up at her with imploring eyes.

"Did you miss us?" She leaned over to kiss the top of the dog's head. "I missed you, too. Should we call Alec and talk to him?"

Sadie seemed to perk up. Jo swore the dog understood English perfectly. She dialed Liam's phone number and let it ring several times before hanging up. The answering machine had clicked on, but she didn't really want to leave a message.

She'd call back in a few minutes. But as she reviewed her list of Gallo names from the phone book, her mind kept returning to Alec and Liam. Where were they? At dinner? Involved in some other recreation? Liam's fiancée had family in the area, too. Maybe they were spending time there. Jo tried not to be envious. If her son was happy, that was all that should matter. So what if he was bonding with a family that wasn't hers? His circle of love could expand from their small nucleus, right?

Right.

It still hurt, though.

Jo reoriented her thoughts and called the next number on her list. No one answered. It seemed everyone had something else to do tonight besides answering their phones. She called the next number.

"This is Stella," a woman answered.

Jo gave her the spiel and then waited for the invariable, "I can't help you," but instead, Stella said, "Did you call yesterday?"

Jo paused and looked at her list of numbers—ones she'd checked off and ones she'd starred to call later. "I don't think so." Her mind raced. "Maybe it's possible. I've tried to keep my notes straight."

"My mother told me someone called asking for Orlando Gallo," the woman said.

"It was probably me. I've been calling every Gallo name in the phone book," Jo said. "But I didn't mean to call the same number twice."

"Ah. We have two lines at the house," Stella said. "Now tell me why you're looking for Orlando."

Jo's thoughts froze. She hadn't expected this question. Did this mean that Stella was a real lead to the man? "A man by the name of Orlando Gallo saved a woman's life when they were both buried beneath a fallen roof during the 1906 earthquake."

The woman at the other end of the phone said nothing, so Jo continued. "Her name is Maggie Howard—well, that's her married name—and she's been looking for him."

"Looking for Orlando?" Stella echoed.

"Yes, to thank him," Jo said. "Maggie said they'd planned to meet up—after their hospital stays. They were both injured, but Maggie never found him after she recovered."

The silence on the other end stretched out, and Jo's pulse drummed fast as she imagined all kinds of scenarios as to why this woman seemed so interested.

They were only on their third day in San Francisco, so was it possible that they'd already had success?

"Is Maggie with you?"

Jo rose to her feet, her heart in her throat. "Yes. She's asleep, but I can get her on the phone."

"Oh, no, don't wake her up," Stella said. "I'm curious, though—how old is Maggie?"

"Ninety-four." This woman had to be a connection—a relative . . . a granddaughter?

"Ninety-four, wow," Stella said. "And she's been looking for Orlando all these years?"

"Yes. Maggie said she tried to find him for months after the earthquake." Jo's voice had gone faint. She should probably sit down again because her legs felt like water. In fact, Sadie was watching her with concern.

"Jo," Stella said. "Is it possible to meet Maggie? I think it would be better if I speak to her in person rather than over the phone."

"Does this mean . . ." Jo was almost afraid to hope. "That you know the man we're looking for?"

"My uncle's name is Orlando Gallo, and he lived in San Francisco at the time. Well, he's technically my great-uncle."

Jo exhaled as tears sprang to her eyes. "Oh my goodness. Wow, Maggie is going to be so thrilled." Her voice broke. "She's been so worried she'd run out of time."

"I understand," Stella said, her voice gentle. "Are you in San Francisco?"

"Yes," Jo breathed. "And you? We can come to you. Wherever you are."

"I think that will be best," Stella said.

They set up a time after Stella gave Jo the address.

When Jo hung up the phone, she sank into the chair, disbelief pulsing through her. What were the chances . . . She leaned her head back and closed her eyes, sending prayers of gratitude heavenward. Stella Gallo . . . Was that her last name? It didn't matter. They'd found Orlando.

Now, Jo debated whether or not to wake Maggie and tell her.

Jo walked into the house, Sadie trotting after her. She opened the door of Maggie's bedroom a crack. Jo stood there a long moment, listening to the woman's soft breathing. A miracle had happened tonight, and Jo couldn't wait to share it. But right now, a quiet peace filled the room, seeping into her heart. And Jo decided to let Maggie sleep.

Morning would come soon enough, and so would the answers.

Jo turned from the room and headed to the back deck. Her heart was bursting, and she wanted to share the news with someone—even Liam. Surely, he'd find the news wonderful, too. But when she called his number, the phone rang and rang, going unanswered.

Finally, after waiting and calling again, but not getting Liam to pick up the phone, Jo reentered the house. She locked everything up and found her way to her bedroom, painted sky-blue, with a white eyelet comforter on the bed. She doubted she'd sleep much at all, but she was going to try to shut her mind off anyway.

Sadie settled on the bed, near her feet, and Jo closed her eyes.

It was good to focus on someone else, and not her own

problems. Maggie was at the end of her life, and she was following her greatest desires—her greatest dreams. Maybe Jo should be doing that—well, within the parameters of being a mom and professor, that was.

She supposed she didn't really know what her dreams were. Finishing her book, yes, but if that was really her dream, she would be spending a lot more time on it. Not just waiting until summer, then finding all kinds of excuses to put it off day after day.

Somehow, she slept, as evidenced when she opened her eyes to sunlight streaming in, with the sounds of breakfast preparations beyond her door. It took only a half-second to remember the phone conversation with Stella the night before.

Jo scrambled out of bed, earning a startled yip from Sadie, and hurried into the kitchen.

Maggie was just sitting down, a cup of tea in her hand. "Good morning. You're a sleepyhead."

"Maggie." Jo braced her hands against the kitchen table. "I found Orlando! Last night, I spoke to his great-niece."

Maggie's eyes widened, and her hands stilled. Her mouth opened, then closed. When she brought her trembling hands to her face, Jo moved around the table and wrapped an arm around her shaking shoulders.

"Stella wants us to come to her home today," Jo said. "She lives in San Mateo. So the drive won't be too long."

Maggie's breathing shuddered, and she lowered her hands. "Am I dreaming?"

Jo met her watery gaze, tears in her own eyes as well. "No, I was going to wake you last night, but then decided to tell you this morning."

"Is he . . . is he alive?" Maggie whispered.

Jo hesitated. She hadn't even asked Stella, and the woman

hadn't said one way or the other . . . "I don't know." Her heart twisted hard. "I didn't even ask. I can't believe I didn't ask!"

Maggie rested a hand on her arm. "We'll find out soon enough."

Jo nodded, but now her tears were for a different reason. She'd been so elated, and now . . . deflated. "I'm so sorry. I should have asked."

"I've waited this long," Maggie said with a soft smile, although the disappointment was clear in her eyes. "I can wait a little longer. It's a true miracle. Thank you for your phone calls. To think that I could have made them all along."

"Let's not have regrets," Jo said. "Let's get ready to go find your Orlando."

An hour later, they were on the road, and anticipation hummed between them. They didn't even turn on the radio. The address led them to an estate in the hills of San Mateo. A winding driveway took them to a sprawling, two-story home complete with pillars and tall, elegant windows. The grounds were breathtaking with their trees and flowering shrubs—everything about this place said peaceful respite.

Jo parked at the top of the circular driveway, then climbed out. She helped Maggie from the car because she guessed the woman would be unsteady, and she was. Jo felt a bit unsteady herself. They walked slowly to the stately double doors at the front of the house.

"Ready?" Jo breathed before she knocked.

Maggie squeezed Jo's arm. "Ready."

Jo knocked, and they waited a good thirty seconds before the door opened. The person standing there was certainly not Stella, but a man in his thirties, Jo guessed. His dark eyes were cool and assessing. Thick, dark hair waved nearly to his shoulders, and he was dressed almost formally. No tie, but his dress shirt and slacks looked expensive, as well as his leather shoes. He was a handsome man; or would be if he wasn't practically glowering at them. The angle of his jaw was held tight, and his full lips were slanted downward.

Jo wasn't sure why she was noticing all of these details, except that maybe she was trying to absorb this whole experience.

"Orlando?" Maggie said.

Jo jolted at the word. Surely, Maggie didn't think this man could be Orlando Gallo. He'd be in his nineties.

"Antonio," the man said, his voice a deep rumble.

He didn't extend a hand or open the door wider. If anything, he looked like he'd have no problem shutting the door in their faces.

"You must be related to Orlando Gallo," Maggie said, her voice clear, if a bit tremulous. "You look so much like him."

The man's face relaxed a tad, but not enough to be considered friendly and warm. "So you *did* know him." Then his dark brows tugged together. "Or have you been looking up newspaper articles on him and have concocted a story that the pair of you were lovers, and now you've come to claim his money for your granddaughter?"

Antonio's dark eyes cut to Jo, and a physical jolt ran through her at the disdain in his eyes. No one spoke to Maggie like that, especially in Jo's presence. This titan of a man was completely out of line. "I'm not her granddaughter," Jo said, taking a step closer to the man. She didn't care if he was the size of a biblical Goliath, she was more than happy to stand her ground. "My name is Jo Sampson, and we're not here to take anyone's money—"

"Toni, Toni, Toni," a woman cut in, her voice honey, with a hint of humor in it. "Are you still carrying on about nefarious women with designs on Uncle's estate? It's been a year since Crazy Annie. Give it a rest, huh?"

If possible, Antonio, or *Toni*, looked sheepish. He moved aside as the woman in question slid between him and the door frame. "Now, which one of you is Maggie?"

The pair either had to be siblings or lookalike cousins. Same dark hair, same coloring, same cheekbones.

"I'm Maggie, and this is my friend and neighbor, Jo."

"Welcome, welcome," Stella said, flashing a warm smile. She was also elegantly dressed, in a peach silk blouse and ivory linen pants. "Sorry about my brother. He's a little possessive."

"Stella—"

She only winked one of her beautiful brown eyes and drew the door open wider. "Come in. We have much to discuss, but the front porch is *not* the place." She blew out a huff of air, as if to emphasize her continued displeasure with her brother. "I hope both of you like an old-fashioned English tea. I spent part of the year in London, and I became quite addicted."

"Where in London?" Maggie was quick to say.

The two women fell into an easy conversation, leading the way through the massive hall, then beyond to an elegant room that opened onto a terrace chock full of planters of fragrant flowers. It was like a miniature Garden of Eden.

Jo almost forgot about the scowling man keeping pace with her as if he were some sort of watchdog for his sister.

A mosaic-tiled table sat in the middle of the terrace, laid with what was indeed a formal English tea. Four places were set, and Jo hid a smile as she thought about Antonio making up the fourth person. He seemed more like a bull-in-a-china-shop type.

Now, *Liam* would have been utterly charmed. Jo tamped down that thought before it could go too far.

"Have a seat," Stella said. "Conversation is always better over food, don't you think?"

Maggie chuckled, even though Jo knew her neighbor must be riddled with curiosity about Orlando. What had happened to him?

Jo stepped to the chair closest to her and was about to pull it out when the chair moved on its own. Well, it was pulled out by Antonio in a smooth gesture. Startled, Jo didn't react for a moment. When he tilted his chin toward the chair, she realized she'd been staring at those dark eyes of his for about five seconds too long.

She murmured, "Thank you," then sat down.

Jo shouldn't be feeling butterflies zooming through her. No, they were absolutely not allowed. She'd been around plenty of handsome men in her lifetime, so why was she having a hard time looking away from this one?

Chapter Eleven

HE ISN'T HERE. MAGGIE could feel it. Surely, if Orlando Gallo was still alive, she'd sense his presence in this home. Although it was beautiful, there wasn't any spry ninety-something-year-old ready to pop out and surprise her.

It was all right, she told herself. More than once. She'd have a good cry later, but right now, she was intent on learning all she could from his niece and nephew. And goodness, Antonio Gallo could have been Orlando's twin. Antonio might be more brusque in his personality, and his voice a lower pitch . . . but those eyes, the shape of his mouth, the straight line of his nose . . .

And Jo was definitely noticing him, too. Maggie felt like giggling over the way her neighbor had a pink flush to her skin. Even if Jo didn't know it herself, it was plain that she found Antonio very, very interesting.

Maggie released a silent sigh. She couldn't blame the woman. Married or not, any woman would appreciate a striking male.

"We're grateful you came all this way to see us," Stella said.

She was a charming woman, and Maggie had liked her from the moment she chastised her brother. In fact, her personality reminded her of Orlando's. Gracious, giving, attentive. Antonio might have Orlando's looks, but the character of the man had been passed down to his great-niece.

"When Jo told me this morning, I couldn't delay another moment." Maggie smiled at her new friend. "We're honored that you invited us, as well. I have been waiting so very long to hear any news of Orlando."

Stella nodded, her own smile sympathetic. "My mother wanted to be here as well, but she had to go into the city for her weekly spa appointment. Nothing can interfere with that."

"Understandable. I hope to meet her sometime." Maggie glanced over at Antonio, who was studying her rather intently. "Are there other nieces and nephews in the area? Or perhaps Orlando's children?"

One of Antonio's brows lifted, but it was his sister who answered.

"No children," Stella said. "Or grandchildren for that matter." She paused, and Maggie didn't know how to read that pause.

"Orlando never married," Stella said, her tone gentle. "But we can discuss that after our tea. Do you like cream or sugar?"

"A little of both." Maggie's pulse was thrumming. For some reason, she couldn't get out the question: *Is Orlando alive or dead?* It was stuck inside her throat.

"I'll have both, too," Jo said, her voice a lot stronger than Maggie was feeling at the moment.

The two women's gazes connected, and Jo gave a slight nod.

"Stella," Jo began, "I don't want to be presumptuous about anything, but is Orlando still alive?"

Stella's hand froze as she was about to pour tea. Carefully, she set down the pot, her pretty brow puckered. "I'm so very sorry. I didn't know that you didn't know." Her gaze cut to Maggie's. "Orlando has been gone for about eight years."

It wasn't a surprise. It wasn't a shock. This is what Maggie had suspected for a while now. He'd lived a good, long life, it seemed. Eight years ago would put him at eighty-eight when he died. And that meant she should have tried harder. She shouldn't have given up so early.

Despite the beauty of the flowers surrounding them and the elegantly laid tea service, Maggie felt as if something dark and hollow was spreading through her.

"Maggie?" Jo said, her voice sounding far away for some reason. This didn't make sense, because they were sitting right next to each other at the table.

"I think she's in shock," another person said. A woman. Stella.

"I can do it." A man's voice. Orlando. No. Orlando was dead. The man speaking was Antonio.

Maggie closed her eyes. It would be better to not see any of this, to not even interact with his descendants. It was too painful. Details she'd forgotten about Orlando were flooding back, and she felt like she'd never truly grieved all these years. Now, only now, was the pain real. What it should be.

"Maggie?" Jo spoke again, and someone was touching her face.

Maggie opened her eyes. She was no longer sitting at the table but lying down. On a couch? A bed? She stared into Jo's light brown eyes. "What happened?"

"You fainted," Jo said. "How are you feeling?"

"I fainted? I never faint."

Jo smiled. "Now you have, and you must rest for a moment. Don't sit up too fast."

Maggie exhaled, then shifted her gaze. There was Stella. And Antonio. Both staring down at her. Antonio's expression was no longer hard, no longer suspicious. His features had eased into concern.

Maggie lifted her head and winced immediately as the fogginess returned.

"Just rest." Stella grasped her hand. "I'm afraid that I've given you a bit of a shock."

"It's not a shock," Maggie said. Why did she feel so very tired? "I mean, Orlando would have been a very old man if he were still alive."

Stella nodded, but one of her brows had cocked.

"I know, like me," Maggie finished. "Don't think I can't see the irony."

"I should have said something from the beginning," Stella said. "I'm sorry that I didn't think—"

"Please, it's all right," Maggie cut in. "I think I've known for a while, but I didn't want to admit it." She looked over at Jo, and in her eyes, she saw her own disappointment. Even if she'd felt like he was gone, she'd still hoped. And Jo certainly understood that. They'd been together nonstop for the past three days.

"I'm sorry I've been a bother," Maggie said, trying to rise again. This time, her mind stayed clear, and she sat up on the couch.

Jo quickly settled next to her and grasped her hand. "There's no rush."

"Here, have this," Antonio said, holding out one of the delicate teacups. It looked like a child's toy in his hands.

Maggie hadn't even noticed him disappearing then reappearing.

"Thank you," she said and took a sip of the now lukewarm tea. She didn't mind. The minty taste had enough sweetness to make her feel even more restored. "Now, where were we?"

Stella shook her head, but she was smiling. "You really did know him, didn't you?"

Maggie wasn't surprised by the question. She supposed the siblings would want some sort of confirmation or proof. But she only had her word. And her memories.

Jo's hand tightened around Maggie's.

"He was so much like you," Maggie told Stella.

The woman's eyes widened. "Me?"

"I agree," Antonio said in a rumble. He'd taken a seat on the wing-backed chair across from the couch, his long legs extended in front of him. "She's naïve and too generous."

It was said in a teasing tone, but Stella's eyes flashed hot. "Hey. I'm a college-educated businesswoman."

"So you are," Antonio said. "But you're still too—"

Stella held her hand up, and her brother obediently quieted. "What else do you remember about him?" she asked Maggie.

"He was an artist, as he told me," Maggie said. "But he was also a storyteller. During the time we spent buried beneath the rubble, he kept my mind distracted and entertained. He had a real gift."

Stella was nodding, and tears touched her lashes. "I remember his stories. In fact, he told us stories about the earthquake, too. And . . ." She glanced at Antonio, who gave a slight nod. "About you, Maggie. He told us about you."

Maggie blinked against hot tears. First, she'd fainted, and now, she was crying. It might take a while to recover from this event. Thankfully, Jo was keeping a tight grip on her hand. Maggie needed all the support she could get. What had Orlando said about her? What did Stella and Antonio remember?

Regret had begun its slow pulse, threatening to turn into grieving. This was an emotion Maggie couldn't afford right now. Not when she had to learn all she could—information she could dissect later.

"Do you think you could walk with me to the other side of the house? I have something to show you," Stella said.

Maggie nodded. She was feeling stronger and clear-headed. The tea had been a good move on Antonio's part. With Jo's hand still in hers, Maggie stood, and the pair of them followed Stella. Antonio joined them, walking behind, and keeping quiet as he let Stella take the lead.

"Orlando had this house built in the forties," she said, "and back then, he must have been thought a movie star or an international importer. But he was never a public figure."

The halls gleamed with the early afternoon light coming in through the floor-to-ceiling windows, which framed a spectacular view of sycamore trees and immaculate garden sections.

"This home is breathtaking," Jo said. "His art must have done well, or maybe he was in another type of business?"

Stella paused before a set of ornate double doors in a deep mahogany finish. "His art did very well."

Maggie frowned. How was that possible? She'd scoured the world, literally, looking for paintings by Orlando Gallo.

Stella pushed the doors, and they both swung open. For a moment, Maggie stood rooted. The interior room was large and spacious, bathed in pale gold light, but that wasn't what caught her attention. Maggie had been to dozens of art galleries in her lifetime, but this room was the most exquisite gallery she'd ever seen. Rising from the floor were sculptures of men, women, and children. Most of them were in poses of everyday tasks. A fisherman with a small boy by his side. A young woman, hand to her pregnant belly, as she held her other hand to shade her eyes. An older man stooping to feed pigeons that had congregated about his feet.

Maggie knew this work. She knew these sculptures because they were miniatures of the originals.

"You have a gallery full of Luca artwork?" Maggie said, releasing Jo and walking into the room. She did a full spin. Other, smaller rooms branched off from the main room. Paintings graced the walls—landscapes, portraits, but mostly scenes of village life and city life, zeroing in on the details of lives lived, loves lost, and joyous reunions.

They were all . . . "Luca," Maggie breathed. She looked over at Stella, who remained by the door, watching. "Did Orlando know Luca?"

"Orlando *was* Luca," Antonio said, his voice rumbling through the spacious room. "He used his middle name as his artist's signature. It helped him be more creative, he said. To step outside himself."

Maggie brought a hand to her mouth. All of this time . . . she'd been searching, when she had already found him.

Chapter Twelve

JO WASN'T AN ART expert, but it wasn't hard to decipher that she was standing in the midst of artwork that had to be world-renowned. The emotion from each piece had its own story to tell, its own emotional journey.

Orlando Gallo, or Luca, was a man whose talents could have only been gifted by a higher power.

"I own a painting in this series," Maggie said, pointing to a large gilded piece on one of the walls.

"Which one?" Stella said, crossing to stand beside Maggie.

"A Child of My Own," Maggie said, her tone tremulous. "I bought it after . . . after I'd miscarried."

Jo studied the current painting on the wall. It was of a mother and infant. The mother was looking down at her child with absolute love and peace. In the background of the painting, a depiction of an angel hovered. Jo wasn't sure if that meant the child was being delivered from heaven, or about ready to be taken back.

"I'm sorry for your loss," Stella said. "Orlando never had children of his own, and I think this series was something expressing what he might never have."

"It's like he can see right into another person's soul," Maggie murmured.

Jo glanced over at Antonio. He had walked into the room and stood by the fisherman sculpture. His expression was unreadable, but the hard lines of before were gone. Suddenly, Jo wondered if he was an artist, too. Or what about Stella herself?

"I can't believe Orlando is Luca," Maggie continued. "I mean, I can believe he is this talented of an artist, but I can't believe his work was right in the open, all of this time."

Stella rested a hand on Maggie's shoulder. "I'm glad you're here now. I think Orlando would be pleased if he knew of your visit."

Maggie took a shuddering breath. She began to move among the paintings and sculptures, spending long moments studying each.

Jo didn't know where to look at first—it was all amazing. She paused in front of the sculpture of an old man bending to feed pigeons. Her eyes tracked the lines on the man's face, the detail of a mole on his chin, the heaviness of his neck . . .

"That was my grandfather," Antonio said.

She hadn't even noticed him standing next to her. Jo glanced up at him. "Was he Orlando's brother?"

"Brother-in-law."

Jo nodded. There wasn't a lot of resemblance between the man and Antonio. "Do you paint, too? Or sculpt?"

Antonio's mouth twitched, and he folded his hands behind his back. "A little."

Jo raised her brows. "I know so little about the artist's world, so you're going to have to explain what 'a little' means."

Antonio's dark eyes focused on her, and she thought she saw a spark in them. Was he angry? Or laughing at her? Or simply annoyed?

Maggie and Stella were now on the far side of the gallery discussing another painting, and Jo suddenly felt self-conscious standing nearly alone with this man and his confusing personality and ridiculously good looks.

"It means . . . that I'm an artist to a very small circle of family and friends, but no one in their right mind would pay for it."

Was this man serious? Or modest? Well, she doubted he was being modest. "You're a tortured artist, then?"

"Something like that."

"Can I see something of yours?"

He regarded her for a long moment, and she'd almost given up on him answering when he said, "Maybe another time."

The heart was a strange thing, because, at the moment, her heart leapt and fluttered as if it alone were looking forward to "another time." But that was ridiculous. Jo was in full control of her emotions and her heart, and her hopes and dreams—whatever those might be.

It was a good thing she had plenty of distractions right now, like looking at amazing art, even if she felt Antonio's gaze on her more than once. She'd simply ignore it. So what if the man was proving to be different than his first impression?

"Come," Stella said, her voice carrying across the expanse of the room. "I've got something to show the both of you."

Curious, Jo left Antonio's brooding presence and caught up with the women. She noted that Antonio wasn't far behind the group, either. A winding staircase that Jo hadn't noticed in the corner proved to be Stella's destination. They all walked up the narrow stairs, single file, Antonio bringing up the rear.

When Jo stepped onto the second floor, she immediately understood why no one was speaking. She was quite speechless, too.

The room wasn't exactly small, nor was it large, and it smelled of turpentine and oil paint. Along one wall was a long shelf and probably a half-dozen paintings, all of the same woman.

Maggie.

That wasn't all, though.

Another wall held larger paintings, ones depicting the devastation of the 1906 earthquake. The detail was exquisite. Smoke billowing from crumbled buildings. People huddled on corners. A crying child. A woman alone in the middle of the street, her expression forlorn. Maggie, again.

Then Jo's gaze was drawn to a sculpture in the corner of two people. They huddled together, the woman's head resting on the young man's shoulder. Their hands were interlocked, a show of strength and faith, amid the rubble that surrounded them. Bricks and debris had been painstakingly sculpted into reality.

Even with Maggie's current wrinkles and aged body, it was clear she was the young woman in the sculpture. And the young man? A youthful version of Antonio. Thinner about the shoulders, and a more narrow chin, but they were certainly related.

"Orlando called this room Maggie's Place." Stella's voice was quiet, reverent.

Maggie walked toward the sculpture, and when she reached Orlando's form, she knelt beside it. She folded her hand over his sculpted hand.

Tears slipped down Jo's cheeks at the sight. Her chest hitched with a threatening sob, and she had to close her eyes to keep control. This was Maggie's moment. Jo didn't need to let her emotions run away from her.

"He looked for you, you know," Stella said. "*For years,* he told me. All during that time, he painted, he sculpted, but he never sold anything. When he finally decided to take his work public, he used his middle name. He said that he didn't want you to find him and have regrets. He believed that you'd moved on, and he was happy for you."

Stella paused.

"I don't think he ever quite got over you," she said.

Tears slipped down Maggie's cheeks.

And Jo found herself wiping her own tears that wouldn't stop.

Maggie was in her own world now, lost in long-ago memories, but the expression of sorrow, regret, grief, and love all made it hard to watch.

Antonio handed Jo a handkerchief, and her first thought was who carried handkerchiefs on their person in 1981?

Her second thought was that she needed to let Maggie have some privacy. The moment felt too intimate, too sacred, even though Jo had been on this quest with Maggie.

"Excuse me," Jo whispered to no one in particular.

Maggie didn't seem to hear her, and that was all right. Jo hurried down the stairs, gripping the curved railing so she wouldn't slip in her haste. She continued past the paintings, the sculptures, the work of an artist who'd lived a full life. Alone. Pining after a woman he would never see again.

Where was the justice in that?

It was a tragedy, pure and simple. The weight of it wasn't even hers to bear, yet she felt it all the same. She had to get herself in control, master her own emotions so that she could be the strength to lean on for Maggie once they left this house.

Jo continued out of the gallery and walked along the hallway, past one room, then another. She had no idea where she was going, but she needed to pass the time until Maggie was ready to leave. Jo stopped in front of a set of French doors that led to a terrace, the same place they'd sat before Maggie had fainted. The tea things had been cleared—by another member of the household? Or did they have staff? Maybe a cook?

This entire estate was immense and beautiful—a place Jo could never dream of occupying. Visiting had been quite overwhelming enough. She crossed to the railing that overlooked a small pond. Enchanting, all of it. But sad, too. She saw that now. There was sadness in the beauty of this place, and it almost hurt to be surrounded by such grace.

She leaned her forearms against the rail and gazed into the pond. The water was nearly turquoise as it glinted in the sun's rays—even the water here seemed more vibrant and beautiful than anything she'd ever seen.

"Miss Sampson," a man said.

Without turning, she knew it was Antonio. She already recognized the tenor of his voice. She didn't want to face him, didn't want to talk to anyone, for that matter. Time to breathe, and reflect, was what she needed.

But he joined her at the rail. Standing a few feet away, he braced his hands on the railing.

Jo noticed his scent, of all things. Even above the fragrance of the flowers and foliage, he smelled of soap and spice.

"Thank you for the handkerchief," she said, at last, not looking at him. "I don't really want to ruin it."

"You can keep it," he said, not looking at her, either. "I have others."

Silence fell between them again, and a strange thing happened. The awareness she felt for this man moved into something more comfortable. She couldn't explain it. She no longer saw him as a man who was suspicious and defensive. But a man who perhaps hadn't been able to see his own dreams realized. Here he was, with a great-uncle who was a renowned artist, yet not a single person would buy his artwork? Had he tried to sell it? Would it be rude of her to ask?

Jo took a small glance over at him. Antonio seemed lost

in thought, as if he wasn't even aware that she stood only feet away.

Then, suddenly, he turned his head, and their gazes connected.

Was it possible to feel electricity through your body when there was no thunderstorm?

Jo wanted to look away from the depths of his eyes, but she didn't. Or maybe *couldn't* was the more accurate description.

"Is Jo short for something? Jolene?"

"Josephine," she said.

"Ah." He returned to gazing across the pond.

Antonio was certainly an interesting man. Cryptic. Unreadable. "Do you think Maggie will be all right?" Jo said at last.

One edge of Antonio's mouth lifted slightly. "She's ninety-four. I think she has some pretty tough skin."

Jo felt her own smile pressing through at his comment. "She *is* a tough lady. I must agree with you there."

Antonio turned to face her, which made her feel like he was scrutinizing her. Was he?

"How long have you known Maggie?" he asked.

This question surprised her. "Let's see, my son is thirteen now, and we moved into Maggie's neighborhood when he was a baby. She was the first neighbor to welcome us."

"Do you have any other children?"

For some reason, this question felt oddly personal, when in fact, it shouldn't, since she'd just mentioned her son.

"Only Alec," she said. "And you?"

"I have a daughter," Antonio said. "She's eight."

Jo shouldn't have been surprised. He was probably married to a beautiful woman, and his daughter was equally beautiful. She wondered what this towering, serious man was like as a father. Probably something that was none of her business.

Antonio resumed leaning on the rail and looking at the pond. "I don't get to see her as much I'd like, since her mother purposely keeps her very busy."

This definitely piqued Jo's interest. Were they . . .? "I'm divorced," she said in a rush. Why she'd decided to declare that bit of information, she didn't know.

Antonio didn't move his gaze from the pond. "Sorry to hear that. I know how hard that is firsthand."

Now, Jo was even more curious. "Are you divorced?"

He nodded. Then suddenly, he straightened and walked back into the house without another word.

Chapter Thirteen

AFTER JO LEFT, MAGGIE spent the next hour in the room that Stella had called Maggie's Place. Orlando's work was exquisite and breathtaking. Stella had also shown her the adjacent storage room. More paintings. More sculptures. There was simply more artwork than this single gallery could hold. She walked through the cramped storage room, gazing at masterpieces that should be on full display, not shoved in a closet.

When she returned to Maggie's Place, she knew what she wanted to do. She found Stella dusting one of the pieces.

"I need to find Jo," Maggie told her, "and then if you have time, I'd like to speak to both you and your brother."

Stella paused. "Sure. Is everything okay?"

Maggie drew in a breath. "It will be."

"All right." Stella set the dusting cloth down. "Jo is probably in one of the gardens or waiting in the front room."

Maggie followed Stella out of the small room and went back down the circular steps and into the main gallery.

The gallery was alive with form, color, and inspiration. In all of her imaginings, she'd never thought of Orlando's artwork on a grand scale. But here it was. In all its glory. She walked slowly through the gallery to the double doors leading to the hallway. It wasn't like Stella was rushing her or anything, but Maggie needed to find Jo. She wanted to present the inheritance plan to the siblings because she'd changed her mind.

They arrived at the front room, only to find it empty. "If you want to wait here, I'll track her down," Stella offered.

Maggie accepted and found her way to the couch. She sat on the white leather Chesterfield sofa and looked about the elegant space. The furniture was white, the walls a pale gray, and the accents a deep turquoise. It was hard to believe she was in Orlando Gallo's home. She wondered how much he had to do with choosing colors and furniture. She wondered what other hobbies or interests he'd had other than his artwork. He'd talked of his parents and his siblings. All of whom were gone now, too.

Such was the cycle of life.

But seeing what Orlando had created in his lifetime, and being deeply touched by his tribute pieces to her, had given her an idea.

"Here's Jo," Stella said as the two women walked into the room.

Maggie patted the space next to her for Jo to sit.

"What's this about?" Jo asked once she was settled.

"I have an idea, but first we need Antonio."

"Oh right," Stella said, turning, then paused to look at Jo. "Do you know where he went?"

Jo shrugged. "We spoke on the deck for a few moments, then he left."

Stella nodded, then headed out of the room in search of her brother.

"Well," Jo said. "This has been an adventure."

Maggie smiled. "You could say that again."

"I'm so sorry, Maggie," Jo said, grasping her hand. "I'm sorry that you didn't get to see Orlando again."

Maggie nodded. "I am, too, but I had expected this all along. I mean, seven decades is a long time to wait to see someone."

Jo bit her lip, her eyes searching Maggie's. "He really loved you. It was plain in the artwork."

Maggie closed her eyes for a moment. "Surreal, isn't it?" She opened her eyes, feeling the moisture there. "We were strangers when we were buried by the falling roof. From that experience, we both found the love of our lives, but we weren't meant to be together after all."

Jo's hand curled around hers. "Is that what you believe?"

"It's what I must believe." She brushed at an errant tear on her cheek. "Now, I think I have some good news, though, for everyone."

Jo's brows lifted.

Two sets of footsteps sounded outside of the room, and in the next moment, Stella and Antonio appeared.

Antonio looked as if he'd run his fingers through his dark waves multiple times, and his gaze cut to Jo, with questions in his eyes.

Maggie wondered what that was all about—she'd need to ask Jo later.

"Thank you for indulging me today," Maggie said as both Stella and Antonio took their seats. "I know that Jo's phone call probably startled you. But I am so happy to find closure when it comes to Orlando—the man I've never forgotten."

Everyone nodded. Even Antonio looked less foreboding.

"I still am astounded that he dedicated a room to our experience together." Her voice shook as she continued. "He saved my life, you know. Literally. And then he . . ." She waved her hand. "Accomplished so much. I wish I could have celebrated it with him, even if in a small way."

Stella wiped at her eyes, and Jo sniffled.

"I am alone, as you might have guessed," Maggie continued. "I have no children, no relatives younger than me, or older. My aim in finding Orlando's family was to pass on my inheritance to them... to you." Maggie paused at the surprise on both of the siblings' faces. "Frankly, it's substantial. But after seeing how much artwork of Orlando's is stored in closets, I've changed my mind."

Maggie felt Jo's surprise now. "I've decided to open a gallery so that all of Orlando's pieces can be displayed. It's a shame for it to be hidden away from the public. If you want to sell any of it, that's up to you. But I am looking for a manager, since, well, since I'm in my nineties now. Of course, I suppose I ought to ask for permission to display your uncle's work. Should I speak to your mother?"

No one spoke for a moment.

Maggie almost smiled, but then she worried that perhaps she was overstepping her bounds.

Antonio cleared his throat. "I'm the official trustee of Orlando's estate, so my mother doesn't need to be consulted, except to appease her, perhaps. But I'm interested in where you're planning on opening the gallery?"

"Well, in San Francisco. As close to the wharf as possible," Maggie said. "I haven't worked it all out, of course. The idea came to me a short time ago."

"Are you sure?" Jo said. "That's a lot of work, and you should be—"

Maggie held up her hand. "I know it's a lot of work, but maybe one of you would consider being part owner. And then, after I'm gone, you can decide to sell. Or carry on with the gallery and take on other artists or keep it exclusively an Orlando Gallo gallery."

"That is..." Stella began, then looked to her brother.

"Extremely generous," Antonio finished. "The offer is

incredible. Do you want to spend a few weeks making up your mind? This would be a huge undertaking."

"I could spend a few weeks making up my mind, but it's already made up," Maggie said. The moment the idea crossed her mind, she felt the rightness of it down to her bones. "I'd like to spend the rest of this week in San Francisco scouting out locations. That is, if your family is interested in an Orlando Gallo gallery?"

Stella and Antonio's gazes connected for a moment, then Stella said, "We're interested. But if you change your mind, we completely understand."

Maggie nodded. Fair enough, although she wouldn't be changing her mind. She wanted to do something for Orlando, and this was it. He deserved every bit of space in his own gallery. His artwork deserved to be seen, not hidden away in a closet or cramped in a house in San Mateo.

"Jo and I will start working on a list of available locations to visit, and if either of you wants to accompany us, we can keep you updated."

"How about I call an associate of mine who works in commercial real estate," Antonio said. "He can get a list together by tonight."

"Sounds like a great friend," Jo commented.

Antonio shrugged. "He owes me a few favors."

"Excellent," Maggie said. "I have no problem with that, do you, Jo?"

"Of course, not," Jo said.

"I'll go make the call right now," Antonio said, rising to his feet.

Maggie couldn't help but notice Jo's eyes tracking him as he left the room. Was there already a story between the two of them?

"I would love to come as well on your scouting trip, but I

think I'd better start the process of packing up the paintings," Stella said.

"I can pay to hire a crew," Maggie said. "I don't want any of this to be a burden on you or your lovely home."

"Oh, this isn't my home," Stella said. "I mean, I live here now with my mother. She and my father moved in after Orlando's death, then a couple of years ago, my father passed away. Since my mother doesn't like to live alone, I ended up here. And Antonio moved in last year as well. His wife got their home in the divorce, and with all this room, it didn't really make sense to have empty bedrooms floating around. Besides, on the weekends that he gets his daughter, we love having her close."

Maggie was curious about more of the Gallo family tree, but those questions could wait. It seemed she'd already gotten approval from Antonio, the one with the legal power to make decisions, so that was good enough for now. "So it's the three of you living here, with the occasional visit from your niece?"

"Precisely." Stella's smile was soft. "I hope you'll get to meet little Teresa. She was too young to remember Orlando when he was alive, but even she has heard of her uncle's *Maggie*."

The words seemed to strike Maggie in the chest. "It's amazing to think about, that after all these years, he's been *here*. Not too far from where I knew him."

Stella rose and crossed to Maggie, then grasped one of her hands. "Thank you for coming, and thank you for your generous offer of setting up a gallery."

Maggie leaned forward and gave the young woman a hug. Stella was already feeling like family.

Chapter Fourteen

EARLY THE NEXT MORNING, after a night of vivid dreaming, Jo awakened to a ringing phone. She didn't move for a moment, wondering if the ringing was simply an extension of her dream. When it rang again, Sadie uttered a soft woof. Jo darted out of bed and hurried into the kitchen.

The sun wasn't even up yet, but maybe it was Liam—or Alec. Had something happened? Why else would they call so early in the morning? She answered in a breathless voice.

"Hello?"

"Mom?"

Panic whooshed through Jo. "What is it?" she asked, bracing one hand against the kitchen counter. Her thoughts raced from one crisis to another.

"Dad said to tell you we'd be gone all day," Alec said. "We're going hiking and fishing."

"Oh." Jo exhaled as she tried to come down from all of her panicked thoughts. "That's great. It sounds like a lot of fun. You're going pretty early, huh?"

"Yeah, so we can see the sunrise."

Jo stifled a yawn. "I'll watch it, too, how about that?"

"Oh, and Mom?" Alec said. "Krista says that I can stay as long as I want. I could even go to school here. My new friends keep asking me about it."

Jo needed to sit down, but she didn't trust her suddenly blurry eyes to get her to the table safely in the dark. "Oh, wow. I guess that's something to think about. Have you talked to your dad about it?"

"I'm coming!" Alec suddenly said. "I have to go, Mom. See you."

He clicked off before Jo got a chance to say another word. The silence of the dark kitchen surrounded her. Before Alec had left, he'd overheard a phone conversation she'd had with Liam about how long their son should stay for the summer. Jo had brought up how much Krista wanted Alec there, and he'd overheard that portion of the conversation.

Now, it had come back to sting her. In the worst possible way.

She tried to keep her thoughts positive. She shared custody with Liam, and they'd both agreed that he should live with her for stability. When had that all changed? Had this been Liam's plan in the making?

Bitterness heated her body, and she made her way slowly to the kitchen table. She sat down and dropped her head into her hands. Maybe Liam had vetoed it, and Jo was worried for nothing. But her mind was already jumping through the next days, and weeks, and if Alec persisted on this idea of going to school in his father's neighborhood . . .

Jo would be alone. Absolutely alone.

A soft paw nudged her knee, and Jo lifted her head. Sadie must have felt her same emotions because the dog laid her chin on Jo's thigh. She scratched the dog's head. "Hey, girl. Do you miss Alec, too?"

Sadie puffed out a breath, and Jo could swear the dog was agreeing with her.

The kitchen's darkness soon softened to a mellow violet. Dawn was on its way.

"Should we go watch the sunrise?" Jo asked the dog. They headed outside onto the back patio. She sat on one of the chairs, and Sadie plopped down at her feet.

The birds began to sing first, and Jo told herself to enjoy the moment and the beautiful city and the adventure she was on with Maggie. Life didn't turn out how one expected, and this, too, shouldn't be a surprise. Not after the year she'd had.

Not only had her husband left her, but now her son might, too.

Oh, Jo knew it wasn't the same thing, not in the least. But the pain was real as it pulsed against her heart.

As the sky brightened from deep azure to mellow gray, then bloomed with pink and orange, her thoughts turned to another person who was suffering from not seeing his child. Antonio.

Why Jo was thinking of him, of all people, she didn't know. Many people were divorced, but when Antonio had said he was, it was like Jo felt a connection to him. A connection to his pain. As if they shared the same pain, the same story, the same history.

Which wasn't true at all. Yes, they had something in common. That was all.

Jo sighed, and Sadie lifted her head for a moment.

"I'm all right," Jo told the dog. "I just want my old life back." But even as she confessed to her dog, Jo knew that her "old life" had been far from ideal. Her husband had been carrying on with Krista for months, and before that? She didn't even want to ask if his thoughts had strayed before Krista.

So Jo had been in a dysfunctional marriage without even knowing it. She'd turned a blind eye against any signs—things that she now knew she should have seen. Signs that if she hadn't been so caught up in her own career, mothering her son, and pretending that her life was ideal to outsiders, she might have been able to decipher. And gone to marriage counseling? Would that have helped?

As much as Jo hated reliving the moments when she discovered her husband's betrayal, sometimes the memories and emotions slammed into her heart like a runaway train without warning.

The phone was ringing again, and it jolted Jo from her mounting self-pity. Maybe it was Alec. Maybe they hadn't gone on a hike after all, and he'd changed his mind about living with his dad.

She hurried inside, realizing the sun had completely risen, which meant she'd been sitting outside for a good thirty minutes.

"Hello?"

"Ms. Sampson? It's Antonio Gallo."

It took her a moment to reroute her brain and realize that it wasn't Alec or Liam on the phone.

"Oh, hi," she said. "You can call me Jo." She felt both hot and cold at the same time.

"Is it too early?" he continued, his low voice like a rumbling engine. "I hope I didn't wake you."

"No, no, you didn't." She was practically stuttering. "Sadie and I were watching the sunrise."

"Sadie? Another neighbor?"

Jo smiled despite the somersaults going on in her stomach. "My dog. She came along because, well, it's a long story."

When Antonio didn't comment, she added, "What has you up so early?"

"I heard from the Realtor, and Ernest says he has three places to look at." He paused. "One already had an offer on it, but he's willing to delay that until we can take a look. But we should go as soon as possible. So I wanted to call first thing."

"Oh, wow," Jo said. "Do you think it's worth getting into a bidding war over?"

"I don't know if it will come to a bidding war," Antonio said with a chuckle, "but I think it's worth a look."

Jo's skin warmed at the sound of his laugh. He seemed in a much lighter mood today, something she could tell even through the phone. For some reason, this pleased her.

"All right," she said. "I'll get Maggie up and going. What's the address?"

"I can pick you ladies up," he said. "You said you were staying close to the city, so it will be on my way. Besides, parking can be tricky, as you might already know."

"I do know." Jo wasn't going to analyze the goose bumps on her arms at the thought of spending the morning with Antonio Gallo.

By the time she hung up and had roused Maggie, Jo was too busy to feel the sting of Alec's words earlier that morning. She was actually looking forward to the day, and she was pretty sure it had something to do with learning more about Antonio. Was there much harm in allowing a small bit of fantasy into her heart? Maybe talking with him would prepare her for future dating. She assumed that the dating pool for women her age would mean men who'd likely been divorced, too.

After making sure Sadie would have enough food and water for the day, Jo cleaned up the kitchen while Maggie put finishing touches on her lipstick and powder. She really was an elegant lady, and Jo could only hope that she'd be half as classy in her nineties as Maggie was.

Jo wasn't sure what she expected, maybe for Antonio to honk? But the doorbell rang right on time, and Maggie got there first. So by the time Jo came out of the kitchen, Sadie trailing, Maggie had greeted their guest.

He was dressed more casually than yesterday but still looked classy in his pale blue polo and khaki slacks. He wore loafers with no socks, which made him look like he should be on a yacht advertisement—with that dark, wavy hair of his that looked slightly mussed, and the golden tan of his skin.

Sadie moved ahead, and before Jo could reprimand her, the dog had pushed her nose against the hand Antonio held out.

"Is this Sadie?" he asked.

Sadie yipped, and wagged her tail furiously.

"Nice to meet you," he said, giving her head a good scratch.

Sadie leaned against Antonio more, pushing all of her weight into him so that he had to take a sidestep.

"Go easy on him, Sadie," Jo said. "You act as if you never get any attention."

Sadie, of course, ignored her and only pushed against Antonio again. He continued scratching her, and she slid to the floor in ecstasy.

"Not much of a watchdog against strangers," Maggie quipped. "But she's good company."

"Any attention is a good day for Sadie," Jo said, her gaze connecting with Antonio's when he lifted his eyes. He was definitely a dog person, and that made Jo wonder if there were any pets at the Gallo estate she hadn't noticed.

"She can come if she wants," Antonio said, now shifting to scratch his new best friend's belly.

"It's all right," Jo said. "She's not the most obedient dog, if you haven't already noticed."

Antonio smiled then, and Jo almost had to put her hand over her heart to slow the impact. His brown eyes sparkled with warmth, and Jo found herself smiling back. A moment passed, then two, and when Jo's cheeks started to heat, she distracted herself by calling to Sadie.

The Healing Summer

"Come on, girl," she said. "Let's go in the backyard and get your ball."

Sadie leapt to her feet and bounded through the house in pursuit.

"Well, that was easy." Antonio was still smiling.

Jo really had to break her gaze from him. "She loves that old ball of hers." She hurried after Sadie before the dog pawed the back door into a pile of wood shavings. Antonio's chuckle trailed after her, and Jo found her pulse doing all kinds of crazy jumping jacks.

She opened the back door and shooed Sadie outside. Then she tossed the ball once for her before saying goodbye. As she walked to the front room, she schooled her features and ordered her blushing cheeks to cool off. This was a morning of touring some real estate, and not mooning over some incredibly handsome guy who smiled like an Adonis.

Maggie linked arms with Jo as they headed down the porch steps. Jo almost stopped short when she saw the sleek convertible in the driveway. The cherry red was bold and beautiful. Reminding her of the owner.

"I thought I'd bring Orlando's favorite car," Antonio said.

"This is beautiful," Maggie said. "What is it?"

"A 1964 Aston Martin DB5," he replied as he opened the passenger door. "Orlando babied this thing."

Maggie shook her head. "I didn't know he was a car man."

"Oh, he most definitely was."

"I'll sit in the back," Jo offered before Maggie could climb in. It would be safer that way for a myriad of reasons.

"Now, I could put the top up, ladies," Antonio said. "Or leave it down. Your choice."

The edge of Maggie's mouth lifted. "Let's keep it down, shall we?"

"Would you like me to get you a scarf?" Jo offered.

"No, I want to feel the wind in my hair."

Jo had to laugh at that. She didn't mind the wind, and now she knew why Antonio's hair had been ruffled.

With everyone settled in, Antonio backed out of the driveway, his gaze moving to the rearview mirror. Jo's eyes connected with his briefly, and she looked away quickly. As Antonio drove along the neighborhood road, Maggie was all smiles and kept throwing joyful glances at Jo.

The morning temperature was perfect, and the car purred along the quiet streets of San Francisco. In an hour, they would be all a bustle, but right now, the golden reflection of the rising sun and violet shadows made the city look like its own painting.

It wasn't long before Jo was smiling, too.

Chapter Fifteen

MAGGIE WAS SMILING, BUT tears moistened her eyes as they neared the wharf. She didn't know if it was the exquisite car that had belonged to Orlando or sitting next to his great-nephew, but Maggie could feel her old friend's presence. She imagined him smiling at her, his brown eyes full of the twinkle she remembered. She'd only seen him briefly before and after they'd been buried in the rubble, but they were images she'd never forget.

Antonio slowed the '64 Aston Martin in front of a building that Maggie could only describe as full of windows.

"Which one is this on our list?"

"It's at the top." Antonio parked against the curb, then turned off the purring motor. "I thought we'd see the best first, then go from there."

Maggie nodded. "Fair enough." She used the side view mirror to pat a few things into place. Antonio was quick to make it to her side and open her door. She appreciated the gentlemanly gesture.

He held out his hand, and she grasped it to stand and steady herself. "Thank you," she murmured.

Antonio only nodded, then stepped forward to offer assistance to Jo in climbing out of the car. She didn't need it, but she acquiesced anyway, and Maggie didn't miss the flush on her friend's face. It was as Maggie suspected. Jo found some attraction in Antonio, and no one could blame her. After all, they were both single. Maybe not both available, emotionally, but perhaps spending time with a charismatic man like Antonio Gallo would crack some of the ice that gripped Jo's heart.

The young woman needed some light and laughter in her life. And the company of an elderly woman and a dog could only help so much.

Maggie turned to look up at the building. She wondered if both stories were available, or another business occupied the second floor.

"Here's Ernest," Antonio said as a dark green Volvo pulled to the curb behind their convertible.

The man who stepped out of the Volvo was extremely thin, accented by the pinstripe of his navy suit. He removed his aviator glasses and smiled broadly, which turned up his well-groomed mustache.

"Toni! What a treat!" Ernest stepped forward and embraced Antonio, then turned to the women.

"Which one is Mrs. Howard?" Earnest looked from Maggie to Jo as if he truly didn't know who the elderly one was.

"Call me Maggie," she said, sticking out her hand.

His smile widened. "Then call me Ernie."

They shook hands, then Ernie turned to Jo. "You must be Ms. Sampson."

"Jo," she quickly corrected.

"Thought so." Ernie winked.

Interestingly enough, Antonio frowned at his Realtor friend. But Ernie didn't seem to notice.

"Well, shall we, ladies?" Ernie said, his tone peppy. He strode to the front doors and produced a key with a flourish. Then he unlocked the door and pulled it wide to allow everyone to enter ahead of him. "She's a special place, if you ask me. In fact, you'll see for yourself."

Ernie's pronouncement proved to be true, because the moment Maggie walked into the first floor and saw the vaulted ceilings and the effect the multitude of windows had on the lighting of the place, she knew this was what she wanted.

Maggie stood a moment in the center of the room while the others milled about. From here, she could see the wharf through the windows. The early morning joggers, the businessmen and women in a hurry, the sun playing on the bay . . . It wasn't the exact location where she'd met Orlando, but it felt like it could be.

This empty room represented a composite of the old and the new. A place where old memories mixed with new possibilities. Orlando might be gone in body, but there was no reason to think he was gone in spirit.

"Maggie?" Jo said, touching her elbow. "Are you all right?"

Maggie blinked and focused on Jo's brown eyes. "I'm fine, dear. Isn't this place remarkable?"

"It is," Jo agreed. "Ernie wants to show us the upstairs. Do you want to see it?"

Maggie took another glance out the tall windows. "Yes, of course." She walked arm in arm with Jo, following Ernie up the staircase that had seen better days. But the place was impressive regardless of the upgrades that would have to be made. When they reached the top of the stairs and walked into the main room, Maggie's breath caught.

The windows were high enough that they overlooked a good portion of the bay, giving the view that appeared in several of Orlando's paintings. It was as if he'd painted from this very room.

Maggie released Jo and walked slowly toward the bank of windows. The men's voices became background noise because all she could focus on was the undulating San Francisco Bay and the early morning fishing boats. The blue of the water was almost impossible to describe—definitely an artist's mixture of hues.

Jo came to stand by her, but she said nothing, as if sensing that Maggie wanted to be alone in her thoughts. And she was. Orlando would have loved this place—Maggie could feel it down to her very toes. He would probably tell her it was too expensive, but then he'd be persuaded. How, Maggie wasn't sure, but if he were alive, she knew she'd be able to convince him.

She drew in a long, steady breath, then clasped her hands.

Turning, she caught Ernie's gaze as he was pointing at a light fixture and explaining something to Antonio about the wiring.

"What questions do you have?" Ernie asked, dropping his hand and striding toward her.

"My only question is when can I sign the paperwork?"

Ernie didn't even look surprised. "Did Toni tell you I have another buyer who's made an offer?"

"Has it been accepted?" Maggie asked pointedly.

"Not yet," Ernie said. "The offer went in yesterday, and the seller hasn't reviewed it yet."

"Then add mine to it," she said. "While you're at it, increase the bid by ten percent."

At this, Ernie did look surprised. "You don't even know what the other offer is."

Maggie smiled. "It won't matter."

Ernie adjusted his jacket's lapels. "Very well, ma'am. I'll have it ready in no time and sent over just as you've requested."

Antonio joined the group, a frown marring his brow. "Don't you want to see the other locations?"

"Do they overlook the bay?"

Ernie shook his head.

"Then I don't." Maggie gave Antonio a sweet smile, then reached for Jo's arm. "I'd like to go walk the wharf now. Maybe find a nice place for brunch."

"All right," Jo said, although her tone was one of suppressed surprise. "If that's all right with Antonio? Or we could catch a taxi back to our rental."

"I'll come along," Antonio said, the edges of his mouth lifting.

"Well, then, very good." Ernie stuck out his hand and shook Maggie's, then Jo's, then Antonio's. "I'll show you out, and I'll be in touch as soon as possible."

Maggie nodded and began walking toward the stairs. Once she reached the bottom, she felt a little jolt in her heart. She was doing something good, something important, she knew it deep within. And it was an amazing feeling.

She and Jo headed toward the front door and stepped onto the sidewalk. The modern city had been completely rebuilt, and nothing was left of the 1906 disaster. Time really was a healer of all things. As they waited for Antonio to wrap up his conversation with Ernie, Maggie leaned close to Jo.

"Do you mind that we prolong the morning with Antonio?"

"No," Jo said, her brows tugging together. "If you'd like, we can send him on his way."

"Oh, no," Maggie said. "I enjoy his company, and I think you do, too."

Jo released a light scoff. "Don't tell me you're getting ideas. Just because you fell in love with his look-alike doesn't mean that I'm under that same spell."

Maggie pressed her lips together to keep from laughing, but some of it spilled out anyway. "Am I that transparent?"

"Very," Jo said, but she didn't sound bothered in the least.

"He seems like a nice man," Maggie continued, keeping her voice low. "And he's handsome."

Jo looked like she wanted to roll her eyes. "He's not really my type. Besides, I'm not dating, especially someone who lives in a different state."

"What is your type?"

Jo bit her lip. "Well, the more academic type, I guess. Like my ex-husband. Someone who runs in the same circles."

"Opposites make better marriages," Maggie declared. "As you've experienced." She wondered if she'd crossed the line, but wasn't able to find out because Antonio was approaching.

"Ready?" he said.

Maggie smiled. "Lead the way."

"Oh, no," Antonio said. "This is your day. I'll follow you ladies."

"All right, then," Maggie said. "Let's walk on the other side of the street until we see a restaurant that strikes our fancy."

They'd only walked a block when Maggie stopped, her gaze focused on the building across the street. It was the same location where she'd last seen Orlando. The building was different, of course, rebuilt and sturdy. But the corner was the same.

She'd been here before, of course, but today felt different. She knew that he'd lived until just eight years ago. She knew that he'd dedicated paintings and sculptures to her. She knew that he'd never forgotten.

Jo and Antonio must have sensed that she needed a few

contemplative moments, because they didn't question her or speak at all. The three of them stood together, gazing at the building.

In years past, Maggie's heart had always been heavy when she visited San Francisco. But this morning, there was a new lightness inside of her. She smiled and grasped Jo's hand and squeezed. Then she grasped Antonio's warm one.

Chapter Sixteen

JO COULD TELL THAT Maggie was ready to call it a day. They'd walked for an hour along the wharf, stopping to eat, then more walking. She told Antonio about some of her memories of Orlando, and Jo had never seen a more attentive listener. Well, except for the moments Antonio had glanced at her. Which had happened several times.

Now, they were heading back to the rental house. Maggie's carefully coiffed hair was looking ragged, and new lines seemed to have appeared on her face.

"We can go to the estate for the afternoon," Maggie said, "and help Stella sort through the art pieces."

Antonio glanced over at Maggie, surprise in his gaze, echoing the same surprise that Jo felt. Maggie never seemed to slow down.

"Maggie," Jo said, leaning forward in the convertible. "Why don't you rest and spend time with Sadie? I'll take the car over to the estate and help out for a few hours, then bring some dinner back. Tomorrow might be a busy day if the offer is accepted, and we have to go downtown to sign paperwork."

Maggie opened her mouth, then closed it. Finally, she nodded, her eyes sparkling. "All right. Maybe you can ride with Antonio if he doesn't mind bringing you back."

"I don't mind," Antonio said at the same time that Jo said, "I'd prefer to drive."

She ignored the jump in her pulse at his offer—she wasn't quite ready for all that alone time with him, and never planned to be.

"It's settled, then," Maggie continued. "However you want to get there. I'll keep Sadie company."

Jo was pretty sure Maggie thought she'd pulled off a major matchmaking heist, but it was far from that. She needed Maggie to be healthy and rested. This was *her* project, not Jo's.

Antonio's gaze connected with Jo's in the rearview mirror, and his lips curved. She glanced away, not wanting to know what he found so amusing. She could guess, and that was enough. She didn't need to share secret smiles with a man who was too handsome for his own good. Or for *her* own good.

Antonio pulled into the driveway, then said, "Do you want to follow me over?" His brown eyes were warm today, and Jo nodded.

What was the harm in following over in Maggie's car? At least Jo would have her own transportation and not have to be one-on-one with the man. "Let me check on the dog, then I'll be out in a moment." And freshen up.

She went into the house with Maggie.

Sadie was more than happy to bestow her energy upon Jo. "Be good for Maggie," she said. "No whining or barking."

Sadie's ears drooped, which made Jo laugh.

"It's nice to see you smiling and laughing," Maggie said, reaching to scratch Sadie, putting the dog straight into ecstasy.

"Haven't I been smiling and laughing?" Jo tried not to let Maggie's comment sting. Had she been a boring traveling companion?

"Not as much as today," Maggie said. "And I think I know who to thank."

Jo suppressed a sigh. "Look, Maggie. I know you're teasing me, but before it goes any further, you know that I'm not interested in dating. And someone like Antonio is not even in my same hemisphere. Plus, we're in different states—"

Maggie clucked her tongue. "You're thinking too much about it all. Have a little fun, Jo. It's all right to find interest in a man outside of your regular life."

Jo wasn't going to get anywhere with this type of conversation, plus Antonio was waiting outside still. "I'm going to see if I can give Alec a quick call, then I'll see you in a few hours."

Maggie only smiled and nodded.

Jo walked into the kitchen and dialed Liam's number. No answer, which probably meant they were still on their hike. It was all right. Really. Alec was having a great time, and that's what mattered most, right?

Jo headed outside into the early afternoon sun. Antonio was leaning against his car, hands in his pockets. Looking like he had all the time in the world.

"Sorry to keep you waiting." She walked to where Maggie's car was parked. "I'm surprised she agreed to stay here."

"I guess you were pretty persuasive," he said, straightening. "Are you sure you don't want to drive together?"

Jo ran a hand over her ponytail. "No, I don't want to tie anyone up. And it gives me some flexibility, in case . . ."

One of his dark brows lifted. "In case, what?"

"Uh, nothing." She gave a faint smile. "We should get going."

She watched Antonio slip into the sports car, then she swallowed over the awkwardness building in her throat. Her heart and mind were running away with imagining what it might be like to go on a date with a man such as Antonio. They probably had very little in common, aside from both being divorced and having a child. That was probably a good portion of the human race, and nothing to dwell upon.

She sensed Antonio was probably driving slower than he preferred so that Jo could keep up. She was already missing the feeling of freedom that riding in the sports car had brought. In a car like that, one could forget problems for a short time. Problems like what sort of conversations her son was having with his dad and future stepmom... Why couldn't Liam's fiancée be someone Alec didn't like?

Jo sighed. She needed to be more mature—more adult—about this all. Her marriage was over. Done. And Alec didn't need to be *her* emotional support. One of her colleagues had gone through a divorce several years ago and had talked about going to a support group for divorced women. Jo had scoffed at the idea—at the time. She had imagined women sitting in a circle, cheap coffee cups in hand, bashing on men in general.

But now... Jo was curious. It didn't take Maggie to tell her that she was holding onto a past, and a relationship, that hadn't been authentic. She still saw her early marriage through rose-colored glasses, and she blamed the *other woman*, when in fact, it had been *her* husband who was the guilty one. It was a hard fact to swallow that the man she'd loved, the man she thought she'd grow old with, hadn't felt the same way.

Jo's eyes were burning with threatening tears. This would not do. She didn't need to be on the verge of crying when she faced Antonio again and walked through his beautiful home.

Up ahead, Antonio turned onto the long drive, the cherry red of his car flashing orange as it caught the sunlight just right.

Jo took a couple of deep, stuttering breaths, trying to draw strength from some forgotten place within.

Antonio parked alongside a silver SUV, and Jo's curiosity piqued. Did Stella have a visitor? Or maybe this was their mother's car?

She parked as well and climbed out. Antonio was waiting for her, but his expression had closed off. He was back to the formidable man she'd first met when he'd opened the door. She wanted to ask him who the visitor was, but she didn't know if that was highly personal.

Antonio strode to the front door, opened it, and said, "I think you're about to meet my ex-wife."

Jo couldn't have been more surprised, but then again, she was at his home. Voices sounded from the direction of the kitchen. Women talking, mixed with a younger, higher-pitched voice. His daughter?

"Come with me," Antonio said. "Stella is probably with them, too."

Jo nearly cringed as the voices turned to laughter. She'd be walking in on family time, it seemed, and with Antonio's guard up, Jo wondered if she should even be here. Were there family issues to sort out? If his daughter was here, why wasn't Antonio more pleased? Surely, he could stand to be in the same room with his ex?

Whatever was going on with the Gallo family dynamics, Jo didn't expect what she saw in the kitchen. A voluptuous woman—who had to be the former Mrs. Gallo—stood at the kitchen counter, chopping vegetables. She was pretty, with wide hazel eyes and an abundance of dark hair with lighter streaks. She wasn't drop-dead gorgeous, as Jo had assumed. Of course, her figure was another matter, and she didn't hide much of her curvy shape with her lowcut summer dress. A young girl sat perched on a chair, her arms around an older woman—the grandmother. And Stella stood at the stove, stirring a boiling pot of pasta.

"Toni," the woman said, setting down the paring knife.

"Papa!" the young girl said at the same time. She wriggled away from her grandma and launched herself at Antonio's waist.

He pulled her close into a hug. "Hello, my *cara*."

"Where were you?" the young girl asked, her face upturned. She was a mirror image of her mother, although her eyes were darker—like Antonio's.

"Just in time for dinner," his ex said, her gaze cutting to Jo. Her smile stretched, and on most people, it would be welcoming. But on this woman, it felt off somehow. "Who's this?"

"Jo Sampson," he said, peeling his daughter away from her clutch and setting her on the stool close by. "Jo, this is Valentina." Then he motioned to the older woman. "And my mother, Gianna."

"Don't forget me!" a young voice said.

Antonio's eyes swung to his daughter. "I could never forget you, *cara*. This is Teresa."

"Nice to meet you all," Jo said, trying to hold onto a genuine smile even though so many pairs of eyes were assessing her. She extended a hand in Gianna's direction. But instead of shaking her hand, Gianna stepped forward.

"We greet like Italians in our home," she said, air-kissing each of Jo's cheeks.

"Yes," Valentina said, her smile tighter as she moved around the counter. The woman air-kissed Jo's cheeks as well, and next, Stella took her turn.

Goodness. Jo felt . . . surrounded. And self-conscious. The women of the Gallo family all wore expensive perfumes. Jo probably smelled like the dog she'd been petting a half-hour ago.

"Are you hungry?" Gianna asked.

"What brings you here?" Valentina said.

"Where's Maggie?" Stella asked.

The three women laughed. "We're going to scare you off," Stella said with a wink.

"Who's Maggie?" the little girl piped up.

While Stella explained about Maggie and Orlando, Jo felt Valentina's assessing gaze on her. Why did she feel like she was on a stage with a spotlight shining down on her?

"Can you fill the wine glasses, Toni?" Valentina said, moving back to the cutting board. "And don't forget which wine is my favorite."

Antonio only nodded. Jo tried not to watch the pair of them and stay focused on Teresa and Stella's chatter.

"Uncle Orlando knew Jo?" Teresa said, her eyes wide.

"No," Stella said. "Jo's friend Maggie."

"Then she must be very old!"

Stella laughed, and Jo smiled.

Valentina had moved to where Antonio was pouring wine at the table. Her long nails skimmed his forearm as she leaned close and spoke quietly.

He flinched and moved around the table.

Valentina smiled, her gaze triumphant.

Jo had to look away—it felt like she was spying on some sort of intimate moment. Even if Antonio seemed put off, his ex-wife was clearly still interested in him. Strange and confounding. Well, not exactly confounding, because Antonio was a beautiful man. This only made Jo more curious about why they'd divorced in the first place.

Chapter Seventeen

THE NEXT TWO DAYS passed swiftly as Jo worked with Maggie and Stella in the gallery at the estate, instructing the movers they'd hired to pack and transport the art pieces. The process took a while, because Maggie had to examine each piece, and she usually had a memory resurface about Orlando that they all listened to as she shared.

It was fun, it was good, except for the way that Jo's heart continued to betray her. Every time Antonio came into the room, either to talk to Stella about something or to help, Jo's pulse went up about three notches.

Apparently, his daughter, Teresa, was staying the entire week at the estate. Her mother had a last-minute trip planned with some girlfriends. Antonio was perfectly pleasant around his daughter, but it seemed the moment she was occupied with something else, his brooding would return.

And Mrs. Gianna Gallo? She was something else. She talked of her former daughter-in-law as if she were still part of the family. Which she was, technically, since she was the mother to Gianna's granddaughter. But that only made Jo's regret all the more pronounced when she overheard a conversation—more like an argument—between Antonio and his mother.

Jo had gone to the kitchen to get everyone something to drink while they worked. She also planned to call Liam's number to see if Alec was around to talk. Since his first hint at wanting to live at his dad's, all of Jo's conversations with him had been cut short for one reason or another. And Jo hadn't wanted to approach the topic with Liam until she knew more from her son.

She stopped outside the kitchen, keeping out of sight, when she heard the raised voices.

"She still loves you, Toni," Gianna was saying. "She's not perfect, but you aren't, either."

"I'm not saying I'm a saint, Mother," he shot back. "And I don't expect my wife to be perfect, but loyalty is important in a marriage."

His mother made a sort of half-cry.

Antonio's footsteps sounded. "I'm sorry. I didn't mean it that way. I'm not *you*, though. My heart isn't as forgiving as yours."

A sniffle.

"It wasn't just that once, you know," he murmured.

Jo brought a hand to her heart. Were they talking about . . .

"I know," his mother said, her voice trembling. "She told me the affair lasted for two months, but that she regrets every moment."

A sigh. From Antonio. "That was the *first* affair."

Gianna gasped. "Valentina told me—"

"Mother," he said in a firm voice. "Valentina told me a lot of things, too. But I had her followed by a private investigator. There was a second affair. That's when I threatened divorce."

"When was that?" Gianna's tone was disbelieving.

"When Teresa was five," he said, disdain in his tone. "I stuck it out for two more years. And two more affairs."

The Healing Summer

"She had more affairs?" His mother's voice had dropped to a whisper. "But I thought things were getting better, and then she was pregnant..."

"It wasn't my child."

The bitterness in his tone felt like a claw at Jo's throat. She knew that bitterness. Had tasted it every day for the past few months.

"I don't believe it." His mother sounded shocked. "Even Valentina wouldn't stoop that low."

"She did," Antonio said. "When she miscarried, she laughed when I expressed my own sorrow. She said that it wasn't mine, anyway, so there was nothing to cry about."

Jo covered her mouth with her hand.

Antonio had gone through so much with the woman who thought she could keep him as a plaything. And they had a daughter together who would forever bond them the rest of their lives.

"I'm so sorry, son," his mother murmured.

Jo turned and headed toward the back terrace. She needed some fresh air. The confession she'd heard was twisting her heart, and she understood Antonio's dark moods all too well now. She couldn't blame him in the least. The pain and bitterness in his voice had been palpable. His grief was far from healed.

The cool breeze coming off the pond was refreshing, and she readjusted her haphazard ponytail. She'd been so focused on working in the gallery that her appearance had been the least of her concerns. She probably looked a sweaty mess, though.

Jo didn't know how long she was on the terrace before someone joined her. They hesitated, then a low voice said, "You overheard, didn't you? I thought I heard footsteps, but I wasn't sure, and then I find you here when you haven't left that gallery for three days."

She couldn't turn; she couldn't face him.

He joined her at the rail, and both of them stared at the rippling water of the pond.

"I didn't want to upset my mother, but she's been so persistent," Antonio said in a quiet voice. "Normally, I can ignore her jabs, but with Teresa here all week, we're together a lot more."

Jo glanced over at him. His hands gripped the railing so tight that his knuckles were white.

"I didn't mean to eavesdrop," she said. "I'm sorry for all that you've had to go through."

He blew out a breath and lowered his head. "I was made a fool twice, and then after that, I only shamed myself. Valentina won't change, and I have to live with that." He closed his eyes. "The worst thing is that I worry about Teresa and how to keep her from growing up to be like her mother."

His words cut right to Jo's core. Antonio had voiced *her* greatest fear. What if Alec turned out to be a cheating womanizer like his father?

She moved to Antonio's side, and without thinking what her actions might mean, she grasped his hand. He didn't pull away, and he didn't act shocked. Then he turned his hand so that their fingers linked.

His fingers were warm against hers, his palm solid, and she swore she could feel the pulse of his wrist beating as fast as hers.

They only held hands for a few seconds, until a sound from somewhere within the house drew them apart, bringing Jo back to reality. She moved back to her place at the rail. "My son wants to live with his dad." She felt Antonio's eyes on her, but she didn't look over at him. If she did and saw compassion there, she might get too emotional.

"He says he has friends in the neighborhood, and they're

asking him to go to school with them." Jo exhaled. "It's not that I don't want him to have a great school year. And I don't resent the time he spends with his dad . . . it's *his fiancée*."

"He's engaged again?"

Jo dipped her head in acknowledgment. "To the woman he left me for. And she's been great to Alec. I think knowing that my son has a relationship with the woman who came between me and Liam is what hurts the most about all of this."

Antonio didn't respond for a moment. Then he straightened. "Want to go somewhere? For a drive? Get out of here for a couple of hours? I think my mother would be grateful for the space."

Jo looked over at him. Was this about giving his mother space, or was this about something more? Her heart rate had already doubled, giving her the answer. "I really should get back to the gallery."

His dark brown eyes scanned her face. Something in his expression sent a warm shiver straight to her belly, and she drew in a breath.

"The gallery isn't going anywhere, and the hired workers can earn their pay."

Jo's breath released. "All right. I'll go tell Maggie." She turned, but before she could take a step, Antonio grasped her wrist.

"I'll tell my mother on the way out," he said. "We don't need to announce it to the masses. They'll find out soon enough."

Jo found herself smiling. "Okay."

"Okay?" Antonio dropped her wrist, but he was close enough that Jo could smell his spice and soap. His mouth lifted. "Let's go pick out a car, then."

Jo had all kinds of questions about that statement, but she held off for now. She walked with him back to the kitchen, where his mother sat at the counter with a cup of tea, or maybe coffee. She looked up, a hopeful expression on her face as her son entered.

Jo hovered in the doorway, unsure of where her place was in all of this.

"I'm sorry, Ma," Antonio said, bending to kiss her cheek. "Can you watch out for Teresa? I'm taking Jo for a drive."

Gianna's eyebrows skyrocketed, and she cut her gaze to Jo.

Should Jo say something? Anything? Nothing?

"We'll be back before dinner," Antonio continued, then he walked toward Jo. Placing his hand on her lower back, he steered her out of the kitchen.

Jo was pretty sure her cheeks were flaming over the way Antonio had announced their excursion to his mother. He dropped his hand within seconds, but the message was clear to anyone who happened to notice. Antonio was interested in her. And she wasn't sure how she felt about that. Or if she could even fully believe that a man like him, beautiful and broken as he was, saw a kindred spirit in her.

Not that she thought he was *romantically* interested. No. But they had a connection. A growing bond. And it couldn't be denied.

Friends. They could be good *friends*. After all, their paths would surely cross if they were both connected to Maggie and Orlando over the length of Maggie's life.

When Antonio opened one of the garage doors, Jo stood back and gaped. The interior of the garage was immaculate, and the walls whitewashed. In neat order, four cars were parked. Not one of them was ordinary or plain. She didn't even know their names, but they were gorgeous.

"What's the yellow one?" she asked, literally unable to look away from the sleek sports car.

Antonio grinned. "You like it, huh? I call her Shirley, and she's a '71 Chevrolet Corvette Coupe."

"Sounds expensive."

This time, Antonio laughed. "She's worth every red cent. I think you'll agree when we're less than a mile down the road."

"We can take it?" Jo asked, incredulous. "It's immaculate. Won't dirt or something get on it?"

Antonio chuckled and lifted a hand to push away a hair that had strayed to her cheek. "You make me laugh, *cara*."

Cara. She'd heard him call his daughter that, and Jo could deduce that it was some sort of endearment. He was already walking away, toward the Corvette, but she still felt the warm brush of his fingertips against her skin.

Breathe, Jo silently commanded herself. *It's just a drive.*

She was soon proven wrong, though. Nothing could be *just a drive* with Antonio Gallo behind the wheel of a sports car.

Once they reached the highway, Antonio opened up the car, increasing the speed. The wind tugged at Jo's ponytail, loosening it until her hair was streaming behind her. She wanted to whoop, or laugh, or shout something as the adrenaline pumped through her veins at the exhilaration she felt.

Antonio drove like he was a professional racecar driver—thankfully not that fast, but fast enough that Jo was out of breath within moments.

He glanced over at her, his eyes light with joy and his smile wide. "What do you think?"

"This car is amazing."

Antonio laughed, but his gaze lingered on her longer than she expected. When he finally refocused on the road, Jo had to reconvince her heart that friendship with Antonio was all that she could, and should, expect.

Chapter Eighteen

THE NEW GALLERY HAD been cleaned professionally over the past few days, and Maggie was thrilled with the progress. Antonio had been more than helpful and had brought in contractors to rewire the electrical lights and make other smaller repairs. The painters finally finished the main floor and were working on the upstairs space now. The wood floors had already been sanded down and re-stained, which explained the sharp chemical smell in the air.

The painters had opened all the windows, along with propping open the front doors. The morning was warming up quickly, but Maggie loved the fresh air combined with the sounds of the wharf mixing in with the morning traffic.

Maggie walked through the empty space of the gallery, which felt cavernous right now, as she planned and sketched in a notebook where she wanted each art piece to go. She'd erased a lot and redrawn the sections. But overall, things were coming together.

"Good morning," a deep voice said behind her.

She turned to see Antonio walk in holding a sack of bagels and a carrier with foam coffee cups.

"Good morning." Maggie smiled at the soft expression on his face—something she'd noticed of late—and she suspected it had to do with his friendship with Jo.

They'd been quite chummy, although Jo had denied any attraction or dating potential. Well, she had admitted she found him handsome and charming—as any woman would. But for the rest of it, Jo seemed determined to hold onto her decision of not being ready to date or enter into any type of relationship.

"Jo's upstairs," Maggie said.

"I'm looking for you."

"Oh?" Maggie laughed. "I'll believe that when I hear what you have to say."

Antonio set the food and drinks down on one of the work tables, which was littered with a measuring tape, rulers, and graph paper. He leaned against the table and folded his arms. "I have a proposition for you to consider."

This was interesting, and Maggie was all ears. She moved toward the table and opened the sack. He'd brought her favorite bagels—onion. "Well?" she said, meeting his gaze. "What's the proposition, Mr. Gallo?"

The edges of his eyes crinkled with the humor she'd seen in him more and more of late.

"I've been wanting to renovate the bungalow on the estate for some time, and now I have a good reason to start on it right away. That is . . . if you're interested."

Maggie lifted her brows. "Interested?"

"In moving here."

Maggie waited a heartbeat. "What gives you the idea that I want to live in the area?"

Antonio unfolded his arms and rested a hand on the table. "You're glowing, Maggie, if you don't mind me saying so. Being around Orlando's artwork has been a touching experience for you, I can tell, and I think it will be more convenient for you to live closer. Be more hands-on with the gallery."

Maggie narrowed her eyes. "Did Jo put you up to this?"

He didn't even hesitate. "We talked."

Puffing out her breath, Maggie drew out a bagel and set it on one of the napkins she had retrieved out of the bag as well. She fished out a plastic knife, then opened a tub of cream cheese. Antonio said nothing as she prepared the bagel. She took a hearty bite, then chewed for a long moment.

Still, Antonio waited.

Moving to San Francisco meant selling her house and deciding what to do with her stuff. She'd taken a tour of the grounds with Stella, and knew exactly the bungalow Antonio referred to. From a logical standpoint, it made sense. Maggie was ninety-four, after all. It was probably time she downsized from her large, stately home. The one that had remained empty of children and grandchildren for decades.

Maggie used another napkin to dab at her mouth, then she sipped some coffee. Finally, she met Antonio's dark, patient gaze. "It's not like we're related, Mr. Gallo. I mean, what will people say when they hear that an unmarried, single woman lives on your property?"

Antonio's lips twitched. "If they're curious, they'll come to see for themselves."

"And what will they see?" Maggie quipped, trying to keep her own expression straight.

"A lovely woman who has worked her way into the Gallo family's hearts," Antonio said. "And it's not because of her money."

Maggie burst out laughing, and Antonio grinned.

"You're a charmer, sir, yes you are," she said. "I don't know how you hold all the ladies off."

His eyes flashed with something Maggie couldn't decipher, but his smile stayed easy. "Think about it, at least. That bungalow needs new life in it, and I've put off the renovation far too long."

"Fair enough," Maggie said. "There's a lot to consider, you know."

At this, his expression turned somber. "I can help with whatever you need. I can arrange for movers and even oversee them."

Maggie couldn't help but stare at the tall, handsome man, who reminded her of Orlando more every day. Not only in his appearance but also in his heart that was bigger than the ocean. "You've already done so much," she said, waving at the space around them as if to prove it. "I'm not sure why you're helping me so much."

Antonio looked toward the windows, his jaw working. Then he spoke in a quiet voice. "That first day you arrived at the house, I'll admit I was suspicious. But when I saw your reaction to my uncle's work, I understood something that I had never realized could be possible."

Maggie waited, the only sounds around them coming from the painters upstairs.

Antonio slipped his hands into his pockets. "I realized that true love existed. Maybe not for everyone, but it had for you and my uncle. It made me realize that I could hope for myself . . . maybe someday . . . to have something close to what you had with Orlando." He looked at her then, and she shouldn't have been surprised at the moisture in his eyes, because her eyes were the same. "Thank you for showing that to me. My parents' marriage was rough, and well, I'm sure you know enough about mine . . ."

She moved toward him and placed a hand on his arm.

He cleared his throat. "So, you see, Maggie Howard, you're family to me. You're the love of my uncle's life, and that's good enough for me."

Maggie leaned in to him and gave the man a hug that he deserved. His strong, solid arms wrapped around her and pulled her close.

"Thank you, Mr. Gallo," she said. "You're not so bad yourself."

His chest vibrated with a chuckle, and he drew away. "Any approval by you, I consider a success."

His wink almost made her blush—as a ninety-four-year-old woman. "Well, sir, you'd better get the woman upstairs some nourishment. I don't think she's eaten yet today. Worrying about that son of hers."

Antonio immediately frowned. "What's wrong?"

Maggie lifted a shoulder. "What's wrong is she's not moving on from that ex-husband of hers. Her son will be fine. She knows he's happy and thriving. She misses him fiercely, but her true heartache is her son spending time with her ex's fiancée. It's all very complicated, and I told her she needs someone to talk to who would understand. A therapist maybe, or . . ." She paused.

His brows lifted. "Me?"

She smiled. "You probably understand some of the feelings she's going through, better than me."

"I do," Antonio murmured.

Maggie could practically see him thinking aloud. She knew this man was good for Jo, but Jo needed to see that, too. Let down her guard. Trust again. If Antonio was anything like his great-uncle Orlando, this man was loyal through and through. Just learning what he'd endured in his marriage and how long he'd stuck it out had impressed Maggie to no end.

Broken hearts could be healed. It was never too late.

This new gallery was a testament to that.

Triumph shot through her as Antonio grabbed one of the coffees and picked up the sack of remaining bagels. Without a backward glance, he headed upstairs. The painters were doing their thing, but Jo had insisted on painting the trim. Maggie was pretty sure the woman was trying to stay as busy as possible.

And Maggie didn't blame her. She'd had days and weeks like that. Just then, a moving truck pulled up at the curb in front of the gallery. Maggie's heart jumped to her throat. It was here—the first delivery. She walked out to the sidewalk and greeted the two men who climbed out of the cab.

They began to unload piece by piece as Maggie directed them.

"The sculptures will come later in the day," one of the men said, his dark brows nearly connected as he gazed about the gallery. "Another truck will bring them since we didn't want to worry about starting and stopping so much in rush hour traffic."

"That's fine," Maggie said, unable to keep a smile off her face. Orlando's paintings were here. Where they belonged. Overlooking the wharf. They weren't even unwrapped yet, but having them leaning against the walls of the gallery was significant.

"We can start unwrapping the paintings and positioning them if you'd like ma'am," the second man said, his red hair nearly the color of flames in the rays of the morning sun lighting the windows.

"Do you also hang paintings?"

"We do," they both said.

The red-haired man continued, "Antonio hired us for all day, so we can do anything you need help with."

Bless that man. She'd hardly had to lift a finger. "Well, then." She turned her clipboard so they could see her rough sketch. "Once we have the paintings unwrapped, I can show you which goes where."

"Excellent," the dark-browed man said.

And they set to work, just like that.

Maggie joined in, too eager to wait. With one of the X-Acto knives, she carefully slit open the wrapping surrounding a smaller painting. As the packaging fell away, the image of two sailboats on the San Francisco Bay appeared. Maggie had seen this painting, of course. Her gaze moved to the signature at the bottom: *Luca*. One word, that was it. How had she missed it all these years?

Never mind that, she told herself and pushed away the thought of so much lost time.

She refocused on the two sailboats, then noticed something she hadn't before.

Was she seeing things?

Had her imagination finally run away from reality?

A man stood on one of the decks; his features were indistinguishable, but he was looking toward the wharf.

Then her heart nearly stopped. In faint brush strokes near the bottom of the piece, where a wharf had been painted in, there was a woman standing on the dock, looking toward the sailboats. She could have been any woman, but the dark gold of her hair told Maggie that it was *her*.

The frame surrounding the painting proclaimed the name as *Brighter than the Dawn*.

Maggie's eyes filled with tears, and she didn't know why. Crying over a picture of two boats was ridiculous. Yet, here she was, tears streaking her cheeks as sunlight glimmered about her. But somehow, warmth surrounded her, and it was like Orlando was whispering the words to her: *Brighter than the Dawn*.

Only now, a long-ago memory surfaced.

He'd told her in their last couple of hours together beneath the rubble of the fallen roof that when he first saw her walking along the wharf, he thought she'd been more lovely and brighter than the dawn.

"Orlando," she whispered. "I miss you, too."

Chapter Nineteen

ANTONIO TOOK THE PAINTBRUSH from Jo's hands, and she immediately protested. "What are you doing?"

"Maggie said you need to eat." He presented a coffee cup and a sack of bagels.

Both did smell good. Jo shouldn't feel self-conscious around the man. He'd seen her mussed and sweaty plenty of times. But right now, she was speckled in paint, and she'd only slept a handful of hours last night. The phone call before she'd gone to bed had confirmed her worst fears.

Alec had been begging Liam to stay at his house during the upcoming school year. When Liam told her that Alec could come to her home for a couple of weeks before school started, then return to San Diego, Jo had barely held back the tears.

She *knew* it wasn't a rejection of *her*. But it sure felt that way. And had she imagined the triumph in Liam's tone?

She'd cried and agonized half the night. This morning, she'd told Maggie to put her to work, anywhere and doing anything. So that was how she ended up painting with the hired workers. And getting her favorite t-shirt hopelessly spotted. Obviously, Antonio looked excellent this morning, as always. He wasn't in a t-shirt, having painted for two hours already. Yet Jo knew this man would look good in anything or in any state.

Was she staring too much at his dark chocolate eyes and the scruff on his jaw telling her he hadn't shaved this morning as usual? Or maybe she was staring too much at the way he moved with ease, his athletic body effortless in everything he did. What *did* he do? She'd never asked what his job was—although she assumed it had something to do with the estate. She didn't know what he did for recreation—aside from driving incredibly fast in beautiful sports cars. She hadn't wanted to know more about him than she already did, because then . . . then she'd care. And she couldn't let herself care. Caring was too painful.

"I'm not giving the paintbrush back until you've eaten an entire bagel," Antonio said.

She blinked, pulling herself out of her runaway thoughts. With a sigh, she reached into the sack and pulled out a bagel. She didn't bother with the cream cheese, but simply bit into the warm, chewy goodness. Then she took a sip of the coffee. It was decent and still hot.

"Thank you," she said. "I hope Maggie's not ordering you around too much."

Antonio tilted his head as he studied her. Why was he gazing at her like . . . like he was both amused and concerned at the same time? The painters were on the other side of the room, not paying attention at all, but Jo felt like she was warming up from the inside out from Antonio's gaze.

"Maggie's an amazing woman," he said in a low tone. "I'm pretty much wrapped around her little finger now. So . . . if that means delivering breakfast to her neighbor, then that's what I'll do."

Jo's mouth twitched into a smile.

"Want to take a break?" he asked.

"I don't have time for a cruise in whatever sports car you brought today."

Antonio chuckled, but his gaze was still intense. "I was thinking of a walk. Get some fresh air from all this painting."

The windows were wide open, but yeah, the fumes were quite strong.

"Maybe in a couple of hours?" she said. "I'm kind of on a roll here."

Antonio looked around, a line between his brows. "I think we should go on a walk before it gets too hot." His gaze returned to hers, intent again.

"Fine." Jo took another bite of her bagel, then began to wrap it up.

"Oh, no," Antonio said. "Bring the food with you. Remember, you're on orders to eat the whole thing."

Jo barely refrained from rolling her eyes, but inside, she was feeling lighter. The hard work had been good, had been a way to work out her angst and get through the day, but a walk would be nice, too . . . She just wouldn't think of what spending more one-on-one time with Antonio might mean to her already jumpy heart.

She pulled the bagel back out, and Antonio smiled.

"Very good, *cara*."

That endearment struck something deep inside of her every time. She wasn't about to tell him to stop saying it, though. No, it was her secret pleasure that maybe when she was back in Seattle, in a too-big Victorian house by herself, she could remember Antonio's sweetness with fondness.

Antonio took her coffee from her so she could get down the stairs without incident, and once they reached the main floor where Maggie had been working that morning, Jo stopped in astonishment. Along the floor, a dozen paintings had been unwrapped and propped up. They might not be in their places for display purposes, but they definitely looked at home. Maggie was in the middle of directing a man with red hair how high up to measure for hanging a painting.

"We've already had a delivery?" Jo crossed to Maggie.

The older woman turned, her sea-colored eyes sparkling. "Yes, what do you think?"

Jo made a slow turn, taking in the propped paintings. "I think you're an inspired woman, Maggie Howard."

Maggie's laugh was light and lilting. "I'll accept that statement, but I won't take all the credit. This man here has been a wonder."

Jo didn't need to ask who she was speaking about, because she wholeheartedly agreed that Antonio Gallo had been a wonder and a blessing.

"It looks wonderful already," Antonio said, before leaning down and kissing Maggie on the cheek. "We hate to leave you, but I'm stealing Jo for a bit."

Maggie obviously had no problem, shown by the grin that spread across her face. "Take your time."

Jo was going to comment, but Antonio enclosed her hand with his and tugged her toward the door. Her heart stuttered at his touch, and then again when he didn't drop her hand.

So, they crossed the street, hand in hand, Jo's pulse on fire. She could barely swallow down the next bite of bagel, and when she finished, Antonio handed over the coffee cup. Again, not letting go of her hand.

They walked along the wharf. Antonio had been right. The morning was already getting hot, although the cool ocean breeze kept the intensity of the sun tempered. Jo wondered how she could feel so alive and so content at the same moment when last night had been pure agony. Maggie had been right. This man was a wonder.

Finally, Antonio led her to one of the docks, where they

watched sailboats coming and going. She let go of his hand and crossed to a trash can to throw away her coffee cup. When she rejoined him, he'd moved to a railing and had propped his forearms on it. The view was spectacular. Blue, blue water, sailboats, and a mellow, salty breeze. The sounds of the busy street behind them were muted by the sounds of the harbor. She leaned against the rail. He didn't try to take her hand again, and she didn't know how she felt or didn't feel, about that.

"Have you ever been sailing?" Antonio asked. The first words he'd spoken since they left the gallery.

Jo smoothed some of her hair behind her ears as the wind seemed to swirl about them at that moment. "Not exactly. I went on a deep-sea fishing trip once. Our entire faculty made a day of it."

Antonio glanced over at her. "What did you think?"

"I stayed below deck the entire time in a fetal position," she said. "Apparently, I get seasick."

"Ouch," he said with a wince.

"Yeah. I'm assuming sailing would be a bit more aggressive?"

"Depends on the boat."

"Right." She laughed. "Even I wouldn't fall for that."

He only smirked.

"Tell me, Antonio, what is your job?" Jo asked. "You run the estate, but beyond that."

He glanced over at her. "Remember I said I was sort of an artist?"

She nodded.

"Well, my lack of ability led to a different avenue. I'm an art agent who matches collectors with buyers. Work on commission, although I've built up a strong clientele, which pays for the occasional sports car."

"I'll say," Jo teased.

Antonio gave a nonchalant shrug, but his half-smile was smug.

A seagull landed near their feet. Antonio straightened, then reached into his pocket and pulled out a small packet of sunflower seeds. He opened it and tossed the seeds. Soon, a dozen seagulls were congregating around the bits of seeds.

"How did you happen to have sunflower seeds in your pocket?" Jo asked.

Antonio cast her an amused glance. "I put them there."

"For you, or for the birds?"

"The birds, of course."

She folded her arms. "Were you planning on walking the wharf this morning?"

Antonio didn't hesitate much, but this time, he did before saying, "Yes."

"With *me*?"

He turned to her then, the sun's rays changing his dark, wavy hair to nearly bronze. He was dressed more casually than she usually saw him, not that she was letting herself notice Antonio Gallo in well-worn jeans and a polo shirt that emphasized the broadness of his chest.

"A man can hope."

She kept her arms tightly folded because this was definitely flirting territory. They were two adults, and Jo didn't want to mix words or create unspoken expectations. If there was one thing her divorce had taught her, it was that.

"Look, Antonio," she said in a quiet tone. "I live in Seattle, and you live here. You're amazing like Maggie said. But I—" She broke off because the growing sadness in his gaze was hurting her own heart.

Antonio moved close and grasped both of her hands. "Neither of us can predict the future, and I, for one, don't want to. So let's enjoy this day. And the one after. When you return to Seattle, I hope we can still be friends. You'll want to visit

Maggie when she moves here, and," he shrugged, "perhaps take a stroll on the wharf once in a while."

Jo nodded numbly, mostly because she couldn't find any words. That was what she wanted, too, but even more—more that she couldn't have. Not now. Maybe not ever.

His warm thumbs stroked over her wrists, and Jo was pretty sure every part of her body broke out into goose bumps.

"What do you think, *cara*?" he said, his voice low, as if he didn't want even the seagulls to hear. "Can we remain friends, although you live in Seattle and I live here and both of our hearts have been broken beyond repair? Friends are good, don't you agree? Everyone needs one."

"I can do that," she managed to whisper. "Be your friend."

With Antonio's hands clasping hers, and the wind gently tugging at her hair, he leaned down until he was only inches away. She knew what he was going to do at that moment, and perhaps she should have stepped away. Instead, she lifted her chin and closed her eyes.

Then waited.

She didn't wait long, and she heard him chuckle lightly before his mouth covered hers. He didn't pull her close, didn't shift his hands—it was only his lips against hers.

The kiss was light, but it lingered. Much longer than a kiss between "friends" should last. But Jo didn't mind. Her senses spun and collided against each other as she breathed in this man, his spicy soap mixed with the salty breeze and heat of the sun. Leave it to Antonio Gallo to kiss her for the first time in the middle of the day in the heart of San Francisco.

He drew away too soon, and at the same time not soon enough. Jo wouldn't have minded a few more moments. When she opened her eyes, he was smiling down at her.

"I'm so glad we're going to be friends," he whispered.

And, she found herself smiling back.

Chapter Twenty

MOVING DAY WAS EXHAUSTING, Maggie decided, so it was a good thing this was her last move in her lifetime. And, she hadn't done anything, except worry about everything. Antonio had told her to take a final walk through the house when everything was gone.

"You'll regret it if you don't," he'd said over the phone the night before. She'd been chatting with him several times a day as he updated her on the moving details. He'd planned it all. Down to the hiring of the movers, and the selling of her home.

Jo had helped her stage the home—well, Jo had done most of the work. Maggie had just ordered her around. Since returning to Seattle three weeks ago, her neighbor had been quiet. And Maggie had stopped teasing her about Antonio. Jo's son was home now, and it was obvious that she was trying to keep the kid entertained and busy.

But it wasn't working.

He talked continually of returning to his father's neighborhood and attending school with his new friends.

Maggie had felt the pain of Jo's frustration as if it were her own. Alec had been a dear and helped her sort through some things, and she let him take whatever he wanted from her donation pile. Which amounted to some toy collector cars of her husband's.

She peered out the window of the bare kitchen when she heard the rumble of the moving truck start up. A chill spread through her as she watched the thing drive away with all of the earthly possessions that she'd decided to hold onto. The rest had been donated or given away. Except for her Lincoln. That had been transported to her new home as well, although she didn't know if she'd have use for it again.

Maggie turned from the kitchen window and did what Antonio had suggested. She walked through the house one more time. The bedroom she'd shared with her husband, the office, the day room, the library... Without children, they had plenty of spare rooms, but they'd all been utilized one way or another. The house felt like it did the day she and Bruce had moved in. So bare, yet the memories were now a part of the house, too.

Once Maggie reached the front door again, she paused and looked back. The graceful staircase and the chandelier would be appreciated by the new owners now. She stepped onto the front porch and pulled the door shut, locking it for the final time. Tonight, she'd stay at Jo's place, and tomorrow, she'd take a plane to San Francisco.

Maggie hitched her purse over her shoulder and made the short walk to Jo's elegant Victorian. Alec had already fetched her overnight bag earlier that day. She knocked on the door, thinking of the day several weeks ago when she'd knocked and invited Jo to dinner. So much had happened since then, including Maggie finding a best friend in the woman.

The door swung open, and Alec stood there. "We're making cookies for you," he announced, then slid away, leaving the door open.

"That's nice." Maggie walked in. Sure enough, the smell of baking goodness reached her, and she headed toward the kitchen.

Jo looked up from the counter where she stood, dropping dollops of cookie dough onto a baking sheet. Her smile was quick, but it didn't mask the tenseness about her eyes. Maggie moved around the counter and put a hand on Jo's shoulder. "Smells wonderful. What's the occasion?"

"It's because you're moving," Alec announced, sitting on a stool on the other side of the counter. He propped his chin on his hand. "And because I'm bored."

Maggie felt Jo stiffen.

"Good thing you start space camp tomorrow, then," Jo told her son in an even tone.

Alec looked down at the counter. "That's for little kids."

Jo released a sigh. "We've talked about this. You'll be one of the older ones, but that's great because you'll know the most."

Alec still didn't seem too enthused.

"I've never heard of space camp before," Maggie said. "Can you tell me about it?" She settled on the stool next to Alec.

He began to talk reluctantly, but within a few moments, he excitedly told her about the overnight missions where he would get to sleep in the captain's berth.

"Sounds exciting," Maggie murmured.

Jo threw her a grateful glance.

And that's how the evening proceeded. Alec talking about space camp. Jo finishing the cookies. Maggie eating some. Then they had dinner a couple of hours later—a delicious taco soup that Jo had simmering on the stove. When Alec finally went to bed after a bit of protesting, Maggie was about to call it a day, too.

Instead, she joined Jo in the living room, and they sipped hot tea as the night settled about the neighborhood. Sadie padded in and lay at Jo's feet.

"How is everything going with the gallery?" Jo asked.

"Wonderful, from what Antonio has told me," Maggie said. "He's hired a woman whom I interviewed over the phone. Beatrice has already started as the gallery manager, and she's put out newspaper ads for the opening and gotten everything in pristine order. I'm looking forward to meeting her."

"That's great," Jo said, although the enthusiasm of her words didn't match her tone.

Maggie studied her friend. It didn't take much to notice the heaviness about her countenance. "What's going on, Jo?"

"It's been arranged," Jo said in a soft voice. "Well, it's in the works now."

Maggie didn't need more clarification. This meant Jo had agreed to let Alec attend school in his dad's town. "Does Alec know?"

"Not yet." Jo sipped her tea. "I'll tell him after space camp. I need to prepare myself for his elation." Her laugh was sad.

Maggie set her tea down; she was finished, anyway. "He's a good boy, Jo, and yes, this will be hard on you. But maybe it will also be healing."

Jo's brows tugged together. "Healing? I don't follow."

Maggie hesitated, then said, "You need to move on from Liam, dear."

"And being separated from my son will accomplish that?" Jo's voice rose a notch.

"You'll have a chance to focus on your *own* recovery," Maggie said in a gentle tone.

Jo set her teacup down and leaned forward, dropping her

head into her hands. "I don't care about my 'recovery'—Alec is the most important thing to me."

Maggie clasped her hands together. "Of course, he is. And Alec living with his dad during the school year won't change how wonderful of a mother you are. No one is questioning that."

Jo lifted her head, her eyes red-rimmed. "But . . .?"

"But you're not living your life as you should."

Jo shot to her feet and paced the room. For a moment, Maggie expected her friend to argue, but she only paced. After a moment, she stopped, folded her arms, and gazed at Maggie. "If you were me, what would you do? Looking back, of course, with all your wisdom in love and loss."

Maggie exhaled. Now that Jo was truly open to her advice, she felt the weight of a new responsibility. "I can't make your decisions for you."

Jo released a short laugh. "You were so full of advice a moment ago, and now you're backing out?"

"All right, you caught me," Maggie said, her smile tentative. "What I say is only advice, all right?"

Jo nodded for her to continue.

"I think you need to put your house on the market," Maggie said. "That's the first step. After that, you'll figure out what should come next."

Jo didn't respond for a moment. "We remodeled this house together." Her gaze shifted to the walls, to the floor, to the drapes at the tall front windows. "We even picked out the doorknobs together."

Maggie only nodded.

"But you're right." Jo's gaze returned to her. "I've known it for a while. I wanted to keep the home intact for Alec, so he'd have a familiar place. But now . . ."

She didn't finish the sentence, and she didn't have to. Jo

came and sat next to Maggie on the couch. "After selling my house, then what?" she asked in a quiet voice.

"Keep your heart open," Maggie said.

"This isn't about Antonio, is it?" Jo asked immediately.

"No," Maggie said, and it truly wasn't. "I would never be opposed to Antonio, as you know, but keeping your heart open is more about accepting new changes, and embracing the chance to heal fully."

Jo wiped at her eyes, and Maggie reached over and took her hand.

Jo squeezed tight, and after a few moments, she said, "Thank you, I needed to hear that." She leaned her head against Maggie's shoulder.

Perhaps because of the emotional talk that night, Maggie and Jo both slept through their alarms, so it was with a start that Maggie awakened the next morning to Alec's panicked yelling that they needed to get to space camp.

Maggie dressed as quickly as she could and met the mother and son at the front door just as they reached it.

"Sorry for the rush," Jo said. "Do you have everything?"

Maggie had been rushed, but there had been little to prepare this morning. So she joined Jo and Alec in their car and rode with them to the space center, which was on the way to the airport, anyway.

Alec was upbeat, but complaining about traffic. Maggie kept her amusement to herself. Just yesterday, he was complaining about all the little kids at space camp, yet here he was, eager to get there.

Maggie could see Jo's secretly pleased expression in the rearview mirror as well. Their gazes connected at one point and Maggie was gratified to see the resolve in her friend's eyes. She hadn't had a change of heart but was still determined to make some changes.

After they dropped off Alec at space camp, Jo told Maggie, "I'm going to the Realtor's office on the way home. I was up half the night thinking about it from all angles. You were right. I need to move on, and only then can I be a better parent to Alec. And part of that is letting go of my resentments toward Liam. I can do that much better if I'm not surrounded by our shared memories day in and day out."

Maggie smiled. "It's hard, I know, but it will be much better in the end."

"I'm holding you to that," Jo said with a laugh.

By the time Maggie was settled on the plane, she decided a small nap was in order. She'd done a good deed where Jo was concerned, but she was determined to continue their close friendship, even many miles apart. She would write and call Jo, showing her support, and keep the doors of her new bungalow open.

The plane ride was quick, helped along by a short nap, and Maggie grinned when she saw Antonio and Teresa waiting for her at the baggage claim. Maggie only had her carry-on, but this was a good area to meet.

Teresa bounced on the balls of her feet, holding up a sign that read: *Mrs. Howard.*

Maggie chuckled at the sight, then stepped forward to kiss Antonio on the cheek. The initial sight of him caused a quick pang in her chest at his resemblance to Orlando, but it also made her heart soar to think that Orlando's good heart lived on through his great-nephew and niece.

"Now, what do we have here?" she asked Teresa, who was still holding her sign up.

"We made a sign so you would see us," Teresa said proudly.

"Thank you," Maggie said. "No one has ever made a sign for me."

Teresa beamed even brighter at that.

Antonio picked up Maggie's carry-on, and they headed to his car. Thankfully, he hadn't brought one of his sports cars but had a much more conservative sedan to drive her in.

"Are you staying with your father this week?" Maggie asked Teresa by way of conversation once they were settled in the car.

The little girl nodded vigorously. "My momma has a boyfriend, and they went on a cruise on a big ship."

Maggie jolted at the "boyfriend" word, but she didn't want to question Antonio in front of his daughter. "Aren't you lucky, then? Spending time with your father and grandmother."

Teresa shrugged. "Grandma is too old to play with me sometimes."

"Maybe I can play with you once in a while."

Teresa's dark eyes widened. "But you're even older."

"Teresa," Antonio cut in.

"It's all right," Maggie said with a laugh. "At my age, comments like that no longer bother me. Yes, I am older than your grandmother, but I'd love to spend time with you whenever you're free."

Teresa seemed to consider this, then she said in a regal tone, "Thank you, Mrs. Howard."

From the driver's seat, Antonio nodded his approval.

If nothing, living on the Gallo estate would be entertaining.

Once they reached the beautiful location, Maggie was feeling the effects of travel. Perhaps more deeply than some younger folk. Teresa skipped along as Antonio carried her bag around the house on a walking path. When they reached the bungalow that was positioned in one corner of the estate, Maggie smiled at the changes it had undergone since the last

The Healing Summer

time she'd seen it. The climbing rose bushes had been cut back, the windows had been replaced, and blue shutters added.

Inside, the three rooms—a kitchen, an open living room, and two bedrooms—had been repainted, and the hardwood floors refinished. Antonio had added—or instructed someone to add—new furnishings and rugs. The white and blue theme was peaceful and lovely. Upstairs was a loft and a small office that overlooked the back portion of the estate's sloping lawns and another pond.

Maggie would probably spend most of her time on the main floor.

"The refrigerator has been stocked," Antonio said as Teresa ran to the fridge and tugged open the door.

"See? We bought you food."

Maggie smiled. "Thank you so much, dear. I am fortunate to have wonderful friends."

"Papa says you're like family, so I should call you Aunt Maggie."

Antonio cleared his throat as he looked at her. "That is, if it's all right with you."

Truthfully, Maggie was flattered and honored. "Of course you may call me Aunt Maggie."

Teresa giggled and threw her arms about Maggie's waist. Thankfully, she could use the nearby kitchen table as a bit of support. The little girl was sure enthusiastic.

"Grandma and I picked alllll the flowers."

"They're so beautiful. Thank you." And they were. Vases were positioned about the bungalow. On the kitchen table, on the coffee table, on the dresser in the bedroom. There was probably one in the loft. "Are they from your own gardens?"

"Yes," Teresa said. "We have lots of flowers."

Maggie chuckled, and Antonio smiled.

"Hello?" A voice sounded from the doorway, along with a tap on the wood.

Antonio's mother, Gianna, stepped inside. She looked as elegant as always, her dark hair streaked with gray twisted into a tight bun, wearing a short-sleeved silk shirt and flowing white pants, along with gold-colored sandals.

"Hello," Maggie said.

"Grandma!" Teresa barreled toward her grandmother and gave her a tight hug.

"How is everything?" Gianna asked, looking about as if she were proud of the upgrades as well.

"It's lovely," Maggie said. "Thank you for allowing me to live here."

Gianna's smile widened. "Antonio suggested it, and we all agreed."

Maggie thought she heard the tiniest bit of edge to the woman's voice, but she shook it off. Overall, Gianna was a kind, if opinionated, woman. Much like herself.

"We should let you get settled and perhaps rest awhile?" Gianna asked, still smiling. "You're welcome to join us for a late lunch. Or any meal, for that matter. We always have plenty."

"Thank you for the offer," Maggie said. "I don't want to be a bother, though. I'll let you know if there are times I'll join you."

"Very well," Gianna said, extending her hand to Teresa. "Let's go see what Aunt Stella is up to."

Teresa happily trotted off with her grandmother, leaving Maggie and Antonio alone.

"Thank you again for everything," Maggie told him.

He crossed to her and gazed earnestly into her eyes. "You have the house number, and I'll check in often to see if you need anything. Either Stella or I can take you to the gallery any time you want to see it."

Maggie smiled. "You're a kind man, Antonio Gallo. I can't believe we open in a couple of weeks."

Antonio smiled. "It's already getting attention in the newspapers." He hesitated. "Do you think Jo might come?"

Ah... here was the question he was probably wanting to ask since he picked her up from the airport.

"I hope so." Maggie lifted her brows. "I think she'd appreciate an invitation."

"From me?" he asked, doubt in his voice. "Is that all it will take?"

Maggie squeezed his hand, then released it. "I think she'll come to support me, but in her heart, it will be to see you."

Antonio rubbed a hand over his face. "I don't know about that. I've called her a handful of times, but our conversations are brief. She's good at keeping me at arm's length."

This didn't deter Maggie at all. "Keep at it, Antonio. She's worth it."

Chapter Twenty-One

JO ANSWERED THE PHONE on the third ring after staring at the receiver for the first two rings. It was Liam, calling at their agreed upon time. She'd be picking up Alec in an hour, and she'd wanted to run over everything again with Liam before she did. So this was a call she had to answer.

Answering the phone lately had brought its own stress with it. Antonio had called a few times, and well . . . hearing his voice had done all kinds of crazy things to her pulse. These new emotions had grown stronger over the past few weeks. Which, surprisingly, made her feel more detached from Liam. This was a good thing, she knew, but still unexpected.

She was finally coming out of the fog that was her marriage blended with betrayal and confusion. Then again, it had also brought out new resentments of wondering if this was how Liam viewed Krista when he first met her. If the seed of interest had grown into flirtation, then beyond.

"Hello?"

"Is it still a good time to talk?" Liam asked, ever the polite ex-husband.

"Yes, I'm picking up Alec in an hour, then I'll tell him." She exhaled. "Did you talk to the school?"

"Yes—well, Krista did," Liam said. "They already reached

out to his old school, and things can be transferred over simply. The kids in the neighborhood all showed up last night and told me they want to plan a welcome back pizza party."

Jo bit her lip. Of course, they did, and Alec would love it, and he definitely deserved it. She knew if she let down her guard right now, her emotions would plow through with a vengeance.

"Those kids sound really great, Liam," she said, unable to keep the tremor out of her voice.

"Look, Jo," Liam said. "I know this is hard. You can visit anytime. Krista won't mind if you stay in our guest room, or there's a hotel a couple miles away."

Jo held back a scoff. As if she'd ever stay in the same house as Krista . . . "Thanks for the offer. I guess we'll play it by ear."

"All right, great," Liam said, his tone upbeat.

Of course, it was. He was getting Alec for the school year.

"I'll call you after I give Alec the news." They might have talked about a couple of other schematics, but Jo's pulse was pounding in her ears, and it was all she could do to hold back tears before hanging up with him.

The moment the receiver clicked, Jo's eyes burned hot. She pressed her palms against her eyes. How many times could a person cry about the same thing over and over? She had to get herself together by the time she picked up Alec. He didn't need a grieving, weepy mom.

Sadie walked into the kitchen, sought out Jo, and laid her head on Jo's lap. "Thanks, girl," she said. "You're always here when I need you."

Then the phone rang again, startling her. She picked it up, expecting that Liam had forgotten to tell her something. The deep voice was Antonio's, though.

"What's wrong?" he asked immediately.

She squeezed her eyes shut, wishing the timing wasn't so awful. "I'm fine," she said in a voice that didn't sound fine at all. "I'm just . . . uh, I'll be telling Alec soon that he gets to live with his dad after all."

She heard Antonio's exhale on the other end of the line. "I'm sorry, *cara*."

She drew in a steadying breath. "Anyway, what's up? Did Maggie arrive okay? How is she doing?"

"Maggie is here safe and sound," he said. "I'm sorry about Alec. I know that you were hoping he'd change his mind once he got back home."

"Yeah," Jo said in a small voice. "He's only complained about being bored, though."

"He is a teenaged boy, remember?" Antonio said. "That's what we always tell our moms."

Jo's smile was faint. "Yeah, well, divorce makes things like that extremely complicated."

"I know," Antonio empathized.

And she knew he understood.

"Look," Antonio said, "I don't know exactly what you're going through, but I can understand some of it. If there's anything I can do, I hope you'll let me know."

"What could that possibly be, except distract me?"

"I'm always willing to distract you." His voice was low and sexy, and well . . . tempting.

Jo ignored the gooseflesh prickling her arms. "All the way from San Francisco, huh?"

Antonio chuckled, and that warmed her even more. "You can't miss the gallery opening, and maybe you can stay on an extra day or two. There's plenty of room at the estate, and you haven't tried all the cars yet."

"I haven't."

"No, and we should remedy that."

"We should?"

"Yes, most definitely, *cara*."

Jo was officially blushing. She'd never flirted like this over the phone. It was remarkably romantic. "All right, I'll come," she said, surprising herself, and apparently Antonio, because he whooped on the other end of the phone.

She laughed aloud at that. This man didn't hold back his emotions or thoughts, and it was . . . wonderful.

"I'll pick you up at the airport," Antonio said, and she could practically hear the grin in his voice. "Tell me when."

"I need to coordinate my schedule," Jo said, her heart hammering in anticipation.

"I'll be waiting by the phone for your call."

"You will not," Jo shot back with a laugh.

Antonio chuckled. "Maybe not, but I'll be wishing I could."

"I should go," she said in a quieter, calmer voice. "Alec will be finished soon."

"*Ciao, cara.*"

She hung up with him and dropped her head into her hands again. But this time, it wasn't to cry about her son or her failed marriage. It was to revel in the buzzing moving through her body.

Antonio Gallo might get a second kiss. A *friendly* one, that was. Just because she was going to San Francisco didn't mean she was changing their friendship status. She rose from the kitchen table and walked past the boxes she'd already started packing. The house would go on the market next week, and she'd spent the time Alec had been at space camp packing and de-junking.

It was an all-consuming process, which was exactly what she needed right now.

Once in the car, the closer she grew to space camp, the

more she hoped she was doing the right thing by allowing Alec to move in with his dad. Maybe when all was said and done, Alec would change his mind?

She pulled into the parking lot and waited in the designated pickup place. Other parents were bubbling with conversation, but Jo held herself apart, absorbed in her own thoughts. Was she about to become a part-time parent?

Her heart leapt when Alec emerged from the building in deep conversation with another kid. But the second Alec saw her, he said goodbye and jogged over, his stuffed backpack bouncing against his shoulder. Jo pulled him into a tight hug. "How was it?"

"Great!" Alec said, smiling wide. "I'm starving."

"Of course, you are," Jo said with a laugh, although her heart was already aching. How many more lunches would she fix for her son before he left? "I bought your favorite chips to eat with your sandwich at home."

"Thanks, Mom."

That simple phrase made her want to cry about all the missed contact she'd have with him.

Alec chattered the whole way home, making Jo smile at how much he did enjoy the space camp after all. He ran into the house and hugged a tail-wagging Sadie. "I missed you," he announced to the dog. "Do you want a treat?"

Sadie was never one to turn down a treat.

Once Jo had lunch on the table, and they were eating together, she drew in a breath and said, "Hey, there's something I need to talk to you about."

Alec nodded, one hand scratching the top of Sadie's head, and the other holding his sandwich.

"I talked to your dad this morning, and we both agreed that if you still want to go to school in his area, then you can go."

Alec's mouth opened, then he quickly swallowed his most recent bite. "Really?" he asked, his eyes going huge.

"Really," Jo said. "It's up to you, Alec, and whatever you choose, you will own the decision."

Alec pumped a fist in the air. "Gnarly! Wait until I tell the guys. They're going to freak out." He laughed. "I can't believe it! We're going to rule that school! Nick said we can get our lockers in the same hallway."

Jo shouldn't have been surprised at his enthusiasm and that he'd already started making plans just in case. She smiled at her son's excitement and ignored the pang in her heart. She'd already cried enough today. It was time to be happy for her son.

He suddenly stopped talking, his gaze zeroing in on hers. "Are you going to be okay here all by yourself, Mom?"

She hesitated. It was sweet of him to ask, but . . . "There's something else I need to tell you. I'm selling this house."

It was rather comical when Alec looked about the kitchen, noticing boxes for the first time. "Oh, I thought maybe you were going to have a garage sale." His gaze returned to hers. "Where are you moving?"

"I honestly don't know," she said. "Probably closer to campus. I'll make sure I get a place that has a bedroom for you, so that anytime you want to come visit, you'll have your own stuff right there—ready. And of course, a small yard for Sadie."

Alec nodded thoughtfully. "I'm going to miss you."

Jo couldn't hold back the tears this time. She rose to her feet and walked around the table. Then she pulled Alec into her arms and kissed the top of his head. "I'll miss you, too, but I'll be calling and checking up on you all the time. Maybe . . . maybe I can come out there once in a while when you're too busy to travel this way."

Alec nodded emphatically. "Yeah, and you can meet my friends."

"Of course," she said brightly. Jo hadn't been replaced by a group of thirteen-year-old boys. Not really. She thought of what Antonio said: *I'm always willing to distract you.* She definitely could use distracting right now so she didn't burst into tears in front of her teenaged son.

"And Krista's nice when you get to know her," Alec continued.

Jo wasn't going to dwell on that comment. "I'm sure she is." She continued to the kitchen sink and turned on the water, then filled a glass and drank the whole thing down.

One day at a time, she told herself. Or maybe: *One hour at a time.*

Chapter Twenty-Two

IT WAS A DAY OF goodbyes, Jo decided. She'd dropped off Alec at the airport, feeling like she'd sent her heart to San Diego. And now she was driving to the Realtor's office to sign the closing documents on her home. The Victorian had sold after only four days on the market.

Two more weeks, and she'd have to be moved out of the place and relocated. Although the Realtor, Candy Anderton, had pushed her to buy a smaller home or a condo in one of those newer developments, Jo decided she'd rent for six months to a year. Just to get her heart and mind settled to all the newest changes in her life. What if Alec had a terrible school year and wanted to move back to Seattle?

What if he never wanted to leave, and Jo was able to reconcile herself to moving closer to him? Thus, she decided to stay more flexible—besides, packing on her own and preparing the home to be sold had been enough work to last her a good many years. And she still wasn't finished.

At the Realtor's office, the mountain of paperwork was immense. Liam had already signed his portion when the Realtor mailed him the documents. So it was a bit uncanny to see his signature, over and over, reminding her of when they settled their divorce. Every signature felt like another step away from her old life with Liam and a step into the future—toward what? The unknown, at this point. This afternoon, she'd be returning to the airport and taking a flight to San Francisco, where, yes, Antonio would be picking her up.

The thought of him made her multiple signatures flow a little more freely, and anticipation made her pulse drum. Somehow, the paperwork came to an end, and Jo shook hands with Candy. The woman's blonde hair was teased to perfection, along with her pouty pink lips.

"You've been a doll to work with," Candy said, extending a handshake.

"Thanks for everything," Jo replied.

Finally, she was free. Free of Liam in one way, and free of memories that wouldn't go away. She headed to her car that she'd already prepacked with her carry-on for San Francisco. She'd hired a neighbor to feed and water Sadie. On the flight, Jo tried to read one of the magazines, but none of the articles held her attention. So she ended up gazing out the oval window at the endless blue horizon.

When the airline attendant announced their descent, Jo gripped her hands together. Her palms were clammy, and her mouth felt dry. Was she really this nervous? After the plane landed, it seemed like ages before Jo actually stepped off. She headed to the nearest bathroom to check her appearance. She was having a decent hair day, with her natural waves behaving, and her dress pants and peach blouse weren't too wrinkled. She stopped at the drinking fountain next, then headed toward the baggage claim, wheeling her carry-on behind her.

She hadn't seen Antonio outside of the bubble that was his estate or the gallery and downtown San Francisco. So, seeing the tall, striking man with dark hair and even darker eyes standing in the middle of regular folk was a bit disconcerting. She could hardly believe that this man was *here*, waiting for *her*. Jo's heart was already beating a mile a minute by the time he looked in her direction.

In that first moment, when their gazes connected, and recognition dawned in his eyes, she felt herself fall a little bit in love. The smile that began on his face was gradual, genuine, warm. And it went straight to her heart.

Antonio was only a friend, though.

And she was grateful for that and would stay grateful.

He began to stride toward her, his broad shoulders squared, his chin lifted, his mouth smiling.

"Josephine," he said as they grew closer.

Had her name ever sounded like a sexy caress before? She didn't think so. But with the sound of his voice, and the way he was looking at her, warm shivers traveled the length of her body.

"Hello," she said, a hitch to her tone, right before he leaned down and kissed her.

On the mouth.

It was very, very brief.

But it also felt possessive, intimate.

How did he do that?

Antonio straightened, but he didn't step back. His gaze searched her face. "How was the flight?"

"Good." She shrugged. "I read one of the airline's magazines, but I can't remember a word."

His beautiful eyes crinkled at the corners. "You were thinking of something else?"

"Maybe."

He smiled, and she smiled back. All right . . .

"And what about Alec? He got off okay?"

Jo's feet floated back to earth. "Yes. He was so excited that he almost forgot to hug me goodbye." She laughed, but it was hollow.

Antonio smiled, but she could see the understanding in his eyes. He knew what she was really saying. And she took comfort from that. In fact, so much comfort that she reached for his hand. His fingers enclosed hers without hesitation, and she told herself not to be nervous. With his other hand, he picked up her carry-on, even though it could easily be rolled.

They walked out of the airport together, hand in hand, Jo's heart in her throat for more than one reason. She wished she knew what was going through this man's mind. At her boldness of taking his hand. At everything else.

"Is Maggie bouncing off the walls?" she asked as they walked to the curb, where a row of cars sat parked.

He chuckled. "That might be an understatement."

They walked past a couple of cars. At the end of the line was a silver sports car. Jo didn't need to be told that there was a 99.9% chance this was what Antonio had driven.

"Let me guess . . ." She looked up at the man by her side. "Is that one yours?"

"Yes, ma'am," he said with a wink.

"It's beautiful."

"Of course."

She laughed at that. "What is it?"

"A Jaguar E-Type."

In a moment, he released her hand. He opened the trunk of the Jaguar and loaded her bag. Then he stepped around her and opened the passenger door. Before she could slide into the leather seat, he grasped her wrist. "You're more beautiful than any car ever created."

She wanted to laugh, but something stopped her. Instead, she flushed when he brought her wrist to his lips and pressed a kiss there. Her pulse went up another notch. "You are a charmer, Mr. Gallo."

He lifted his other hand and smoothed a bit of hair away from her cheek. "I only speak the truth."

Even though they were surrounded by the airport bustle and the exhaust of cars and buses, Jo felt like she was in her own little utopia that was made up of Antonio Gallo and exquisite sports cars.

"Well, I think you're beautiful, too," she said. It was the truth.

Antonio didn't smile or laugh, though. Instead, his eyes were somber as he studied her face. "You have a generous soul," he said at last. "And you continue to astound me."

Jo's throat literally ached with emotion. This man should be a poet instead of an art dealer. His hands shifted to either side of her neck, and his fingers grazed her jawline ever so lightly. And then he kissed her.

This one wasn't the brief kiss of an Italian greeting.

This wasn't the kiss of friends, either.

This kiss held a longing that Jo matched when she kissed him back. She slipped her arms about his waist and raised up on her toes, perfectly nestling against him. His mouth was warm and sweet and, oh, she could lose herself completely in this moment.

A bus shuddered by as its brakes shifted, and slowly, the sounds of the airport returned.

Reluctantly, she drew away from him. But she could still feel him, still taste him, still smell him.

Antonio dropped his hands, breaking off all contact. But his gaze was intent on hers, which only made her heat up more, thinking of what had passed between them. It would be completely impossible to pretend that she wasn't affected by him.

"I wish that I could have you to myself," he said, a wistfulness in his tone, his dark eyes holding hers, "but it seems we have a gallery opening to attend."

She nodded, her mind both foggy and buzzing at the

same time. It was a wonder that she was able to slide into the seat and snap on her seatbelt. In seconds, Antonio was sitting next to her. The moment he pulled onto the main road out of the airport, he grasped her hand, then accelerated the sports car until she felt like her heart was flying as fast as the wind.

Chapter Twenty-Three

MAGGIE PRESSED HER FINGERS against the pearl necklace at her throat as the first gallery patrons walked into the building. They were people she didn't recognize, and Antonio had introduced her to a lot over the past few weeks. Had they read about the opening in the newspaper? Heard about it from a friend or colleague? Would it be tacky to rush up to them and ask?

Beatrice, the gallery manager, greeted the patrons at the entrance. The woman was somewhere in her forties, and she was certainly a go-getter. Her bright smile matched her cheerful blonde curls that she'd tamed into a chignon for the evening.

On the far side of the gallery, Jo had set up a table of hors d'oeuvres and drinks. Antonio was currently with her, and they seemed to be flirting. Maggie smiled privately to herself. The pair had done a lot of flirting over the past twenty-four hours, and it seemed that they were good friends, indeed. More than friends, if Maggie were to guess.

Jo, of course, refused to analyze the relationship and kept saying she wasn't ready to date. Maggie was pretty sure her mind was being changed, though.

A group of three people came into the gallery, and

Maggie watched them admire one of the sculptures. It felt good. *This* felt good. Having Orlando Gallo's art on display, here for the world to see and enjoy and draw inspiration from.

Stella soon arrived with Teresa and Gianna, and the three of them headed straight for Maggie.

"This place is so pretty!" Teresa was dolled up with a lavender dress and a matching headband to contrast with her dark hair.

Maggie smiled at the little girl who had quickly wormed her way into her heart. She certainly had her father wrapped around her little finger, too. Maggie set an arm about her small shoulders. "I'm so glad you came, Teresa. Do you want some refreshments?"

"I do!"

The adults chuckled, but Stella said, "Not if they're too messy."

"I'll help her," Maggie said, leading Teresa to the refreshment table. She didn't think even a little girl could ruin something with finger sandwiches or mini-tarts. Besides, all of the sculptures and paintings had been roped off.

Jo turned to them expectantly, Antonio by her side.

Maggie didn't miss that their fingers were interlinked, but Antonio released Jo's hand the moment he saw his daughter.

"Teresa, you look like a princess," he said.

Teresa giggled. "I am, Papa."

At this, Antonio grinned and scooped her close.

Maggie caught Jo looking on, a certain wistfulness in her gaze. Surely, she missed her son. And of course, Maggie was curious of what Jo thought about Teresa . . . If . . .

"Ma'am?" a deep voice said behind her.

She turned to see a white-haired man who was reed-thin and towered over most men in the room, except for maybe Antonio.

"Maggie, is it?" he said, his pale blue eyes full of interest.

"Jack," Antonio cut in. He stepped forward and embraced the man. "I didn't know you could come tonight."

"Plans changed," Jack said, drawing back. "And curiosity got the better of me." His gaze again shifted to Maggie. "I wanted to see what the gallery was all about."

But his gaze remained focused on Maggie. There was something familiar about this man . . . but she wasn't sure what. He was probably about ten years younger than she, and he appeared quite spry.

"Maggie, this is Jack Wentworth," Antonio said. "Jack and Orlando were friends for decades."

Jack nodded, his gaze still on Maggie.

She was starting to feel self-conscious.

Antonio said some other things, but Maggie found she was paying more attention to Jack. And Jack seemed to be paying that same attention to her as well.

Jo merely folded her arms and smiled at them both.

"You're Orlando's Maggie," Jack said again. "I thought you were a figment of his imagination. An angel, maybe. With the way he talked about you, I had a hard time believing such a perfect woman existed."

"Oh, believe me," Maggie said, "I'm far from perfect, Jack."

He chuckled, and it was a warm sound.

Maggie folded her arms. "You'll have to tell me some of those stories."

Jack grinned at this. "That would take a while, but I have the time. What do you think about lunch tomorrow?"

Maggie glanced at Antonio, who raised his hands in surrender. But then he winked.

She didn't know what to think of that. Had Antonio meant to introduce them?

Well, Maggie would never turn down any storytelling about Orlando. "I can make myself available."

"Wonderful," Jack said. "Now, how do I get a tour of this place? Do you happen to know any lovely hostesses who can show me around?"

Maggie held back a laugh. She was sure that Jo was eating up this entire conversation along with Antonio.

"I might know a thing or two," she said. "Why don't you come with me?"

"I think I will." Jack extended his arm for her to grasp.

Well, he was certainly a charmer *and* a gentleman. So, Maggie slipped her arm through his, and they began to walk toward the painting with the two sailboats.

He asked her what brought on the idea for the gallery, and that was an easy enough question to answer.

"I wanted to thank him."

Jack looked down at her. "For what?"

"When I saw all that art of his stacked in closets, I decide to use the money I would have passed along to my kids. You see, I never had children, and I'd rather see the money go toward something that honors Orlando's life."

Jack nodded, astonishment in his eyes. "You're a wonder, Maggie."

She felt her face warm. Goodness, it had been a long time since that had happened.

Jack continued their walk, and they strolled up to the painting. Maggie estimated there were about thirty guests at the gallery right now, so they had plenty of leisure to take their time. Beatrice's laughter and conversation rose and fell as she continued to greet the newcomers. She was definitely earning her paycheck tonight.

Jack released Maggie's arm as they stopped before the painting. They stood side by side and gazed at the two sailboats.

"*Brighter than the Dawn*," Jack said softly. "I remember the day he finished this painting."

Maggie snapped her gaze to him. "You do?"

Jack's smile appeared. "He called me on the phone and told me he'd finished an important painting."

Maggie found herself holding her breath as she waited.

"So I drove to his studio, and Orlando did a little ceremonious unveiling." Jack waved his hand toward the painting. "I knew immediately it was a masterpiece. I mean, the emotion rolling off it practically bowls a person over."

Maggie blinked against the prickling heat in her eyes.

"I asked him what it represented, and Orlando said, 'It represents how it feels to meet the love of your life.'"

Maggie blinked against the burning in her eyes. Even though she had recognized the name of the painting as a phrase Orlando said to her, hearing about the unveiling and his subsequent words only nestled this whole experience of finding Orlando deeper into her heart.

After several moments, Jack told her, "Orlando said he'd never sell it. It's nice to see it on display, though."

The words rocked through her, but she wasn't sad—she was suddenly, sublimely peaceful. "Then I won't sell it, either."

Jack gave a small nod. "I'm honored to meet you, Maggie, and if it's still all right, I'll pick you up tomorrow at eleven-thirty."

"Do you know where I live?"

He flashed her a smile then. "Of course." Turning toward her, he bent and kissed her cheek. Before straightening, he said in a near whisper, "If I wasn't a confirmed bachelor, I'd do everything in my power to woo you. But even from the grave, I've no doubt that Orlando would find a way to interfere."

Maggie stared after the tall man as he walked out of the

gallery. She half-expected him to turn and look at her one last time before stepping into the night, but he didn't.

"Interesting man," Jo said, coming to stand next to Maggie. "Lunch tomorrow, then?"

Maggie looked over at Jo. "I suppose. He seems so familiar, yet that's impossible. I've never met him."

Jo bit her lip. "I have no idea, either. Maybe you met him in some random way a while ago."

"Maybe."

Jo was watching her closely. "But you think he's interesting, right?"

Maggie elbowed her. "Now, don't go down that road."

With a grin, Jo said, "Just giving you a little of what you're always giving me."

Maggie latched onto Jo's arm. "Well, you and Antonio are different," she said in a hushed tone. "For one thing, you're both still young, and for another, your first marriages weren't to the loves of your lives, so there's still a lot of room for improvement."

Jo laughed. "You're incomparable, Maggie Howard."

Maggie wriggled her eyebrows.

"By the way," Jo said. "If you get tired before the gallery closes, Antonio said you could head back with Stella. Antonio and I can stay and lock up the place."

"I'm feeling fine right now," Maggie said, and she was. Speaking to Jack Wentworth had given her a bit of spring in her step, although she'd never admit that to Jo. The woman might get grand ideas. "Thank you for the offer, though."

As Jo walked away to tend to the refreshment table, Maggie wondered if she just wanted alone time with Antonio. She was flying back to Seattle in the morning, and things had been busy for all of them for the two days that Jo had been here. They hadn't even had time for much one-on-one talk.

"He would have been so proud and humbled," Stella said, coming up to stand by Maggie in front of the sculpture of the fisherman.

Maggie looked over at Stella. "Do you think so?"

Stella nodded and wrapped an arm about Maggie's shoulders. "I often wonder what would have happened if Orlando had found you after the earthquake. Well, I guess it doesn't take too much imagination to think that you'd be my great-aunt."

"Perhaps," Maggie said with a smile. "Maybe we would have had a torrid relationship—you know those artist types."

Stella laughed aloud, and a few nearby people glanced over at them with curiosity. "Orlando was pretty much obsessed with you, Maggie." She waved a hand to indicate the rest of the gallery. "You'd have to be obtuse not to notice."

Maggie gave a small shrug. "Perhaps the idea of me was bigger than the reality of me."

Stella frowned. "You mean if you'd found each other, the rose-colored glasses wouldn't have stayed so rosy?"

"Exactly."

Stella was silent for a moment as she gazed at the surrounding artwork. "Nope, sorry. I'm going with my original theory. You would have been my great-aunt."

Maggie chuckled. "I like that theory better, anyway."

Stella squeezed her shoulder. "Well, like Antonio, I consider you family, Maggie Howard. You have been generous to a fault, and you have such a good heart."

"Like I told Antonio and your mother, I don't want to be a bother. After this opening, I'll keep mostly to myself. Your mother has been kind to invite me for meals, but I truly enjoy my independence. I hope that doesn't hurt anyone's feelings. Especially your mother's. I sense she isn't always in agreement with a guest staying in the bungalow."

"You're not an inconvenience," Stella said, then lowered her voice. "My mother is . . . how do I say this? Protective as well as a bit territorial. She mostly frets, and sometimes says things she really shouldn't. But we love her anyway."

"Of course, you do," Maggie said. "And I hope you all know the last thing I want to do is encroach on anyone. In fact, I've hired a driver to bring me to the gallery when I want to putter around here and bother Beatrice."

Stella turned to face her, consternation in her gaze. "You don't need to do that. Antonio and I are always happy to drive you."

"I know," Maggie said, squeezing her hand. "But I like to make my own plans sometimes."

"Yes, yes, I know." Stella winked.

When Stella moved off, Maggie headed up to the second floor. This area was less populated, and she walked to the windows that overlooked the bay, which glowed with the deepening bronze from the setting sun. The view was truly picture perfect. And even though Maggie wished that so much had been different in her life, she didn't regret any of her actions now. It was like the pain and losses of the past were finally healing.

Her heart was now full.

Chapter Twenty-Four

"I'M COMING TO HELP you," Antonio told Jo as they drove through the velvety night back to the estate.

The sports car of the night was a Porsche, and since it wasn't a convertible, it was like she and Antonio were in their own little cocooned nest. Teresa had left earlier with her grandmother, Stella, and Maggie.

Being alone with Antonio hadn't happened this weekend yet, except for the airport pickup. So now, Antonio holding her hand and insisting he was going to help her move was doing all kinds of things to her heart.

"That's ridiculous," Jo said, even though she couldn't think of anything she'd love more—spending more time with him, that was. And maybe having him there to help pack might also get rid of some of the more painful memories. "You have a career here, a busy life, and a daughter. I've already started packing, and it will go quickly once I get back home."

Antonio's jaw was set, though. "Would you turn me away if I showed up?"

She shook her head. "Don't put me in that position. I'd only feel guilty, and . . ."

"And?"

"Don't make this harder than it already is."

Antonio said nothing as he pulled off the neighborhood road and turned up the long drive to the estate. He released her hand as he turned smoothly into the garage, then parked and turned off the engine.

Without looking at her, he climbed out of the car.

Was he upset with her? Would this really be the end?

She, returning to Seattle. Him, staying here.

Sure, Maggie and the gallery would always connect them, but that would be the extent of it. Before she could decide how she felt about all of this, her door opened, and Antonio extended his hand.

He was, of course, a gentleman no matter the situation.

She placed her hand in his and let him help her up from the car, but he didn't release her hand. And she couldn't help but feel a skip in her heart.

"Come on," he said. "Let's walk in the gardens."

Another skipped heartbeat.

Antonio led her through the back door of the garage, and they were soon walking along paths that cut through pristine roses and other flowering bushes. Stars hung low overhead, and the moon was nearly full, casting its ethereal light. His fingers interlinked with hers, and he absently stroked his thumb over her wrist. The heat inside of her only seemed to build.

Antonio still wasn't speaking, but she knew there were dozens of thoughts in his head. She just didn't know what the outcome would be. In the distance, a single light glowed from the bungalow. Maggie must have gone to bed and had left a light on for Jo's return.

She would miss her former neighbor—already had. And it was a bit disconcerting to know she'd be returning to a home empty of her own son. The next time she saw him would be his fall break, and she'd be settled in her new condo.

Antonio turned on a path she didn't think she'd taken before. It led to a circular garden that had a birdbath in the middle. It wasn't an ordinary birdbath, but one that could only be an embellished sculpture by Orlando Gallo.

Antonio came to a stop and turned toward her. In the moonlight, his eyes were positively black, and his hair just as dark. Still holding her hand, he used his other hand to scrub through his wavy hair.

She had to look away from his face so she wouldn't change her mind, because allowing him to come to Seattle would bring him into a part of her life that was full of cobwebs.

"*Cara*," he said in a quiet voice, lowering his hand and brushing his fingers against her jawline.

She had to look at him then.

"I don't think it's a good idea, Antonio," she said, hoping she sounded more convincing than she felt. "It will already be hard enough to say goodbye to you." There, she'd admitted it. He could do what he wanted with that information. But it was the truth.

"Why do we have to say goodbye?" he whispered.

He was so close that she could smell his spicy soap and feel the warmth of his breath.

"You said it already," she said. "We both have broken hearts that are beyond repair."

"I was wrong."

She blinked. "What do you mean?"

"I mean that I was *wrong*," he said. "When I'm with you, I don't feel broken. I feel . . . alive."

Her breath caught. She didn't know if she wanted to kiss him or run through the garden until she reached the bungalow and could shut the door between Antonio and her feelings for him. She opted for the former. She slid her hands up his chest and behind his neck, then she pressed her mouth against his.

Antonio didn't hesitate; it was as if he'd been waiting for *her* to kiss *him*. At last.

As his warm mouth captured hers, she wondered who she was kidding. How in the world was she going to say goodbye to this man? Let him go? He'd been so unexpected, still was, and she sometimes wasn't sure if she was existing in reality when she was with him. But *this* moment was real. His touch. His taste. His beating heart against hers.

When he, at last, drew away, he rested his forehead against hers. "*Cara*, please. Don't end us now."

Her eyes were still closed, and all kinds of emotions hummed through her. Mostly that she wanted more from this man. Her pulse was singing, but her fears were screaming. Exhaling, Jo blocked it all out. Listened. To her heart.

"If you come to Seattle, I can't promise anything," she whispered.

"I'm not asking for any promises," he whispered back. "Only a chance."

And that was how, three days later, Antonio arrived at her front door in Seattle. She'd said yes, and he'd shown up.

Jo had spent the last hour getting ready after a morning of packing and stacking boxes into separate piles of what would go with her to the condo and what would be donated. Sadie had been curious about the packing at first, but now she just lounged and watched the activity through half-closed eyes.

"You're such a help," Jo teased her dog.

Sadie snuffled in acknowledgment.

Then, on a more serious note, Jo added, "I hope you remember Antonio. Remember we talked about you being on your best behavior? No barking or growling."

Not that Jo was worried. Sadie had been perfectly in love with the man at first sight when Antonio had come to their rental house. Jo eyed her dog, feeling momentarily guilty that she was about to lose a great yard. But it couldn't be helped.

When she headed upstairs to get ready for Antonio's arrival, Sadie padded after her. Jo had looked a fright. She quickly showered and changed into clean clothing. With Sadie looking on, Jo painted her fingernails and toenails and spent a little extra time on her eyeliner. "I know, I know," she told Sadie. "I'm going overboard."

Sadie merely blinked.

When a knock sounded at the door downstairs, Sadie leapt to her feet and woofed.

"Now you have energy," Jo mused. She checked her appearance once more. Maybe she'd overdone it, but it was too late now to scrub everything off.

There was a rental car in the driveway and a man on her porch.

Jo headed down the stairs after Sadie, who'd ignored all of her instructions and was now barking at the door.

"Enough, Sadie," Jo commanded. "You know it's Antonio. No more barking."

Sadie sat down, her nose pushing against the crack of the door as her tail thumped the floor.

Jo opened the door, fully expecting to see Antonio there, but not Antonio holding roses.

"Hi," she said. "You made it."

His dark eyes danced over her face, and the edges of his mouth lifted into a smile.

Jo smiled back.

Sadie woofed and pushed her way onto the porch.

Antonio looked down at the dog. "Hello, there," he said as he gave Sadie a hearty scratch.

Jo was already glad he'd come, but she was also nervous, and her pulse was in overdrive. Could she really handle a relationship? Would she get even more burned in the end?

"These are for you." Antonio held out the roses.

"Oh, wow. Thank you," Jo said. "They're beautiful." Even though she shouldn't let her mind wander, she thought back to the last time Liam had brought her roses. It had been their anniversary, a few months before she discovered his infidelity. The Jo back then had been naïve, foolish even.

But these roses were different, much different, because they were from a much different man. She inhaled the sweet fragrance, and when she looked up again, she found Antonio's gaze on her. With Sadie still between them, and in full view of her entire neighborhood, he leaned forward and kissed her.

She smiled against his mouth and half-melted against him. He hadn't shaved, and the scruff of his chin sent a warm shiver all the way to her toes.

"I missed you," he murmured against her lips.

How could such a simple phrase upend her carefully constructed world?

And how had kissing him become a regular part of their friendship? She was fooling herself if she thought they were only friends. Clearly, Antonio was fine with amping things up.

Sadie whined, and Antonio drew away with a chuckle. "Don't want to be ignored, do you?" He reached down and scratched her head.

"You're spoiling her," Jo said. "She'll be your friend for life if you keep petting her."

Antonio winked at Jo. "I don't have a problem with that."

"Come in, then," she said. "I guess I'd better put you to work if you're going to be my dog's best friend. She's been useless with the packing."

Antonio stepped inside, and then he whistled. "This place is fantastic—minus the mess, of course."

It *was* a fantastic house, and Jo would miss it. But it was also the right thing if she wanted to move on with her life.

Watching Antonio walk through the first level of rooms, with his tall frame and dark hair, so unlike Liam, was surreal.

She was looking at the house through his eyes now, and when he complimented the woodwork or any original or upgraded features, she explained the work she'd done. With Liam, of course, but she tried not to mention him too much.

When they reached the narrow dining room, Antonio ran his fingers over the antique dining table. "This is beautiful."

The darkened oak table was intricately carved at the sides, and the chairs all matched—rare, indeed. Of course, right now, it was covered in stacked paperwork she'd signed for the closing.

"I found it at a flea market a few years ago," she said. It had been an overcast summer day, and Liam had claimed a headache. So Jo had taken Alec, and they'd wandered for hours. He'd picked out some vintage toys, and Jo had found this dining table. When they'd returned home, Liam was gone. He'd left a note that he'd headed into the office.

Now . . . looking back, Jo was only suspicious.

"Are you all right?" Antonio said, coming up behind her and placing his hands on her shoulders.

Jo hadn't even realized she'd been biting her lip and staring into space. She blinked and said, "Just a lot of memories in this place. Some harder than others."

Antonio bent close and kissed the back of her neck. "Think of all the new memories you have to look forward to in life." He slid his hands down her arms, then linked their fingers.

She leaned against him, and he rested his chin on the top of her head. His arms moved around her, their fingers still linked. Her back pressed to his chest created a cocoon of warmth—surrounded by his arms and by his spicy soap scent.

"I'm glad you came," she said, her throat feeling raw with emotion.

"I'm glad, too," he murmured against her hair.

Chapter Twenty-Five

MAGGIE HAD CANCELED ON Jack Wentworth because she'd awakened the morning following the gallery opening with a headache that rivaled a lightning bolt from Zeus. She'd taken ibuprofen and gone back to bed. But then the headache lasted a second day and a third.

On day four, Maggie was finally pain-free, and she had to assess the damage of a neglected bungalow. Bless Stella's heart, the woman had brought over a few meals and tried to convince Maggie to see a doctor.

But Maggie had refused. Headaches ran their course, eventually. And she was sure this one was simply the result of the accumulation of so many events in such a short time. Moving in the first place would do anyone in.

Someone knocked at the door as she was wiping down the kitchen counter.

"Maggie? It's Stella."

The woman was certainly persistent.

Maggie headed to the front door and opened it, expecting to see Stella holding a platter of food. Instead, nothing was in her arms, but she was smiling.

"You look better."

Maggie touched the hair that was a combination of a rat's and a bird's nest. "I feel much better."

"Great," Stella said with quite a bit of enthusiasm.

Maggie narrowed her eyes. "Are you here for a friendly visit?"

"Not quite." Stella exhaled. "You have a visitor at the main house. I told him I didn't know if you were up to visitors, but he insisted I check."

"*He?*"

Stella nodded, her eyes gleaming.

"It's Jack Wentworth, isn't it?"

Another nod.

Maggie sighed. "Give me twenty minutes." She shut the door and walked to her bedroom. She didn't want to dress up too glamorous, but she wanted to appear cool and collected. She slipped on a pale gray sarong dress, then pinned up her hair. Next, she donned some comfy slide-ons.

She shouldered a colorful handbag she'd bought in Mexico. Heading out the door, she could hear voices coming from the terrace. Stella's, Gianna's, and a deeper male's—must be Jack's.

Maggie felt light-footed, admitting to herself that she was looking forward to seeing the entertaining man again, and of course, hearing some Orlando stories. Through the trees, she caught a glimpse of his tall form. It was remarkable, really, that he'd been good friends with Orlando. And now, here they were.

She moved toward the terrace steps just as Jack turned, his eyes sparkling when he saw her.

"Ah, good afternoon, Ms. Maggie." His grin was contagious, and she found herself smiling back.

"Good afternoon, Mr. Wentworth."

He practically jogged down the stairs and offered his hand to escort her back up them. What a spry man.

"So gallant," Maggie murmured. "Thank you."

"Are you feeling better?"

"I am." She glanced over at Stella and her mother. "Thanks to these ladies' good care."

"It was nothing," Gianna said in a generous tone. "Headaches are never pleasant."

Well, maybe her tone wasn't entirely generous.

"And you eat like a bird," Stella said, pulling out a chair for Maggie. The table had been set with drinks, sandwiches, and fruit.

"Goodness, it's like I'm a queen around here," she said with a laugh.

"According to Orlando, you are a queen," Jack quipped.

"Thank you, but I'm sure your memories are quite embellished." Maggie smiled at the other women. "How long will Antonio be gone?"

"I'm not sure," Stella said. "He wasn't very specific. Not that he can't make phone calls and do business from Seattle. And it's nice to have a bit of a break from his brooding bossiness."

Maggie chuckled. "He's not that bad, is he?"

"He is when he's your brother," Stella said.

"Or your son," Gianna said, affection back in her tone.

"Where *is* Toni?" Jack asked.

Everyone fell immediately silent, and Jack looked about the table, amusement in his eyes. "Ah, is this a private family matter?"

"Not exactly," Stella said. "He's in Seattle, with Jo."

"Who's Jo?" Jack's gaze was definitely interested now.

The other two women looked at Maggie. "She's my former neighbor, and she was on the road trip with me when we connected with the Gallo family. Antonio is there helping her pack her house."

"Is she moving here as well?" Jack asked.

Gianna took a long drink from her glass.

"She's not," Maggie said. "She went through a divorce, and now she's moving on."

"Ah." Jack looked at Gianna, who shrugged, her lips pressed in a thin line. "And your neighbor Jo and Toni are . . .?"

"Friends," Gianna said.

"Friends," Maggie agreed.

Stella sighed. "They're more than friends, and we all know it. Well, *you* now know it, Jack. And Mother doesn't approve."

Gianna's face pinked. "It's not that I don't approve, it's that Toni's ex-wife wants to get back together. But with Jo in the picture now . . ." Her voice trailed off. "Oh, never mind. It's not like anyone around here cares about my opinion, anyway." She rose from her chair, her cheeks still flushed. "Excuse me."

Gianna headed into the house, leaving a stunned silence in her wake.

Stella tapped her glass. "She doesn't approve."

Jack chuckled. "That was quite obvious. But I thought that Valentina mowed through men like a kid in a candy store. Does Gianna think her son should be punished?"

Maggie was more and more impressed with Jack by the moment.

Stella didn't seem bothered by the deeply personal question. "It's a tricky balance. Mother is close to Valentina, and she doesn't want to think the worst of her. Or she thinks she'll change, maybe?"

Jack turned the glass in front of him as if he were thinking. "I've been alive a long time, and well, zebras don't usually change their stripes."

Stella nodded.

The Healing Summer

"I'm happy for Toni, truly, and your friend, Jo." Jack flashed a smile at Maggie.

"Me, too," Maggie said. "Now, enough about other people. Tell me your Orlando stories."

"My first Orlando story starts when I was a kid," Jack said.

"Oh, you've been friends that long."

Jack's gaze became intense. "Do you not recognize me, Maggie?"

She was surprised by his question. "Something about you is familiar, but I'm not sure why."

His smile was soft as he placed a hand over hers. "The earthquake. Orlando saved me. I was that kid he pushed out of the way."

Maggie stared at Jack—this man—who was that boy. She covered her mouth with her hands as her eyes filled with tears. "Oh my goodness," she whispered. Then she leaned forward and kissed him on one cheek, then the other.

Jack chuckled, and when she finally drew away, he said, "So you see, my stories go way back."

She nodded, taking a shaking breath as she wiped at her tears. "I want to hear them all."

And he obliged. They talked for the next two hours as Jack told Maggie about their friendship. Stella eventually excused herself, so then Jack and Maggie were the only ones left sitting on the terrace. As the shade shifted around them, they moved with it as well.

Jack's stories were illuminating into the life of a man she'd known for such a short time but had felt so deeply bonded with.

"He was good through and through," Maggie mused. "Not only rushing to help people in the middle of an earthquake, but he lived his life like that."

"Yes." Jack had eaten two sandwiches and refilled his glass twice. "And he's doing it again. Helping people."

Maggie thought of the gallery, and all of the people who'd be visiting it over the years, receiving inspiration of their own. "You're right. Everyone who sees Orlando's art will come away better for it."

Jack shook his head. "I meant the fact that Orlando brought us together. I now have a new friend. It's been a pleasure talking to you and remembering so many things."

Maggie tilted her head, studying the distinguished man sitting across from her. "It's been a pleasure speaking to you as well. You don't know how much it means to me to hear about Orlando's many joys and successes in life."

Jack extended his hand across the table. "Friends?"

She smiled. "I wouldn't have it any other way."

Jack winked, and Maggie could only shake her head in amusement. He was a charming man, and perhaps, if they had met a decade or so earlier, she might have been able to talk him out of his established bachelorhood . . .

He rose from the table and dipped his chin. "I hope to see you soon. You have my number, correct?"

"I do."

He smiled his charming grin. "And I'll be stopping by the gallery here and there if you don't mind."

"I certainly don't."

Jack tipped an imaginary hat.

Maggie smiled after the man. He was certainly entertaining. And good company.

Now that she was by herself, she relished in the peace of the pond and gardens that extended from the terrace. The estate really was beautiful, and more than once, she'd tried to imagine Orlando walking about, maybe seeking inspiration for his art. It was a nice image to dwell on.

"Where is she?" a woman's voice screeched, startling Maggie.

She straightened and looked toward the terrace doors where the cry had come from. It wasn't Stella, and it didn't sound like Gianna, either.

"Valentina," a sharp voice said. "Neither one is here. Now, did you bring Teresa?"

"She's at her dance class," Valentina replied, in a tone that sounded about ready to screech again.

And suddenly, the woman was standing in the doorway of the terrace. Valentina's dark eyes were rimmed in red, and her hair was like a tornado about her head. "You . . ." She pointed at Maggie. "*You* started all of this."

Maggie gripped the edges of the table and stood, keeping herself braced for balance. "I don't know what you're talking about."

Valentina raised a manicured hand, her long, painted nail pointing at Maggie. "You're the reason my husband is with another woman. If you hadn't come here, looking for a dead man, none of this would have happened."

Behind Valentina, Gianna and Stella appeared, both of their faces pale.

"Valentina," Gianna said, grasping the woman's arm. "Let's sit down."

But Valentina shook off her former mother-in-law. "Where is that woman? I need to speak to her."

"We told you," Stella said in an even voice. "She's in Seattle."

Valentina's eyes narrowed. "With Antonio?"

"She lives there," Stella continued. "Antonio went to help her move."

"That's not *all* they're doing," Valentina sneered. Her gaze cut to Maggie again. "Your friend is a homewrecker, and you're the accomplice."

Faster than anyone could move, Valentina stepped around the table and advanced on Maggie. Before Maggie could dodge the women, Valentina had grabbed both of her shoulders. "You have to leave. You're not welcome here!"

The woman's grip was fierce, and the fire in her eyes told Maggie she had truly lost all reason.

"What are you doing?" Gianna cried in panic.

"Let go of her," Stella shot out.

"Not until she agrees to leave." Valentina leaned close, her grip digging into Maggie's shoulders. "You will leave today and never return."

"Valentina," Gianna said, closer now. "Release Maggie. *Now.*"

Thankfully, those words got through to the woman.

Valentina whipped toward Gianna. "Don't tell me you're on her side? You can't support Toni in this."

"That's enough." Gianna set her hands on her hips, eyes smoldering.

Stella maneuvered between Maggie and Valentina, then folded her arms and sent an apologetic glance to Maggie.

Valentina gaped. "You think *my* husband should be with that floozy of a woman?"

"Ex-husband," Gianna said, her eyes on fire now. "Toni told me exactly what happened and the number of men you've been with. You had us all fooled into thinking that you'd had one negligent slip-up. And if you weren't the mother of my granddaughter, I'd forbid you to step foot in this house again."

Gianna was out of breath now, her chest heaving with indignation.

Valentina snapped her mouth shut, then looked at Stella. "Do you believe Toni's lies, too?"

Stella's brows shot up. "As far as I'm concerned, you're the one in denial here. D-E-N-I-A-L—Don't Even Notice I Am Lying."

The Healing Summer

The previous pink of Valentina's face morphed to red. Her gaze snapped to Gianna's. "You don't have to forbid me to come here. As far as I'm concerned, I no longer know you. Any of you!"

Maggie stared after Valentina as she swept into the house, her heels clicking like a staccato of fireworks on the hardwood floor.

For a full thirty seconds, no one said a thing.

Finally, Gianna turned toward Maggie. "I must apologize."

Maggie exhaled slowly, trying to release the knotted tension. "You don't need to apologize for another woman's behavior."

"I do," Gianna said, her eyes deep wells of regret. "I have been . . . undermining you. And I've been wrong. When my son first said he wanted to offer you the bungalow, I was not pleased. I thought you were an interloper with an agenda for your friend Jo. And I might have said something to that effect to Valentina. So I am partially to blame for this. Until a few weeks ago, I had believed Valentina's pathetic lies about her marriage." She reached for Maggie's hand. "So if you'll accept my apology, I'd like to start over."

"Of course." Maggie blinked against the heat building in her eyes. She had no grudge against the woman, but getting this all out in the open was very cathartic. "I can't tell you how grateful I am for you and your family."

Gianna pulled her into a hug and kissed both her cheeks. "Like my son says, you're a part of our family. Orlando would have wanted it this way, and so do we."

Stella reached for Maggie's hand and squeezed. "We're grateful for *you*, Maggie. Thank you."

Maggie took a stuttering breath. "Well, now that you've made me cry . . . Does anyone want to visit the gallery with me today?"

Both Gianna and Stella gave their own watery laughs.

"We'll both go," Gianna said, looking to Stella, who nodded in confirmation. "Since Valentina didn't bring Teresa, we have the rest of the day free."

Maggie's brow furrowed. "If Valentina won't come here, how will that work with Teresa?"

Stella waved a hand. "Oh, she's never short on making threats. We'll let Toni handle this one."

Chapter Twenty-Six

"What do you think, girl?" Jo asked Sadie as they walked through the rooms of the condo. The place was haphazard with furniture and boxes, but she could already see the potential. Truth be told, she was feeling excited about this new chapter of her life. Her own place, closer to campus, and the opportunity to meet new people and find a different routine.

Sadie sniffed every corner until she approved.

"Do you like it?" Jo asked the dog.

Sadie's wagging tail was answer enough as she trotted up the stairs to the second level. Jo followed and paused on the landing before the master bedroom. Instead of a king-sized bed, the mattress she'd moved was a queen. A new bed had been in order for a long time, and Jo had the feeling she'd be sleeping a lot better at night now.

Sadie suddenly shot down the stairs and barked at the door.

No one had knocked or rung the doorbell, so the dog must have heard something out on the unfamiliar street. "Antonio's not back yet," Jo called down to her.

Sadie sat in front of the door, her eyes trained on the doorknob.

Antonio had gone to pick up food and bring it back before they started unpacking.

The last two days had been exhausting, but exhilarating at the same time. Spending so much time with Antonio had been surprisingly enjoyable. Not only was he someone she could talk to, and relate to, but he got things done lightning fast. He wasn't opposed to heavy work, and she knew without him, this all would have taken an entire week.

Jo paused by the bathroom and unpacked a few things, hanging the towel on the rack. A single towel. She located her toothbrush and toothpaste. Then put the single toothbrush into the cup holder.

Such was her life now.

Sadie barked from downstairs, and a second later, the door opened.

"You hungry?" Antonio's deep voice resonated through the condo.

Jo headed to the top of the stairs and smiled as she watched Antonio interact with her dog. Sadie listened to him more than she listened to Jo.

"Good girl," Antonio said after she followed one of his commands. He glanced up to see Jo, and his face lit into a smile. His light blue shirt contrasted with his olive skin, making him look heavenly.

Jo grasped the banister. She rather loved Antonio Gallo in this new place of memories. She would be happy to remember him here.

"Thanks for getting the food," she said. "But how many are eating?" There were four bags at Antonio's feet.

"I picked up a few basics for you." He scooped up the bags and headed toward the kitchen, Sadie happily following him.

Jo walked down the stairs. By the time she'd entered the kitchen, Antonio was already emptying the grocery sacks of eggs, juice, milk, yogurt, and fruit. His movements were easy, as if he knew his way around a kitchen.

She tried to think back to any occasion that Liam had spontaneously bought groceries or helped in the kitchen. She couldn't think of a time.

"I feel like I'm thanking you every twenty minutes," she told Antonio. "I mean, is there a limit until you get tired of me?"

He shut the refrigerator door and leaned against it, his dark eyes on her. "Come here."

"Why?"

"Come here."

So she walked toward him, each step making her heart thump harder. The intensity of his gaze was like an electric current. When she was close enough to touch him, Antonio slipped his hands to her hips and pulled her against him.

"I'm not going to get tired of you," he whispered as he lowered his head. "And you can thank me whenever you want."

She rested her hands on his biceps. Standing in Antonio's arms was both thrilling and becoming familiar. "Then thank you for getting me food."

"No problem." A smile flashed across his face before he closed the distance between them and kissed her.

The kiss was very sweet but very short.

"This condo is great," Antonio said, his voice rumbling. "But it's too far away from me."

Jo smiled. "You can always catch a plane."

He released a sigh and moved his hands up her back. "You know, in San Francisco, you'd technically be closer to Alec. It's a short plane ride to San Diego."

"You're not playing fair," she said.

"If that's what it takes," he murmured, pressing his lips at the edge of her jaw.

Jo closed her eyes and breathed in this man. There were

too many maybes in her life. What if Alec ended up hating living with his dad and wanted to move back in with her? Besides, she had a career here—had taught at the college for years. She had colleagues, students, a life . . .

Her stomach rumbled, and Antonio chuckled.

"Let's get you fed."

It was nice to be worried over by another person, Jo decided as they sat at the table and ate the still-warm takeout Antonio had bought.

Sadie's mournful eyes stared at the grilled chicken on Jo's plate until she finally gave in and offered her some. When she caught Antonio looking at her with amusement, since she'd told him more than once no table food for the dog, Jo said, "It's moving day, so I relaxed the rules a little."

Antonio just winked and returned to his meal.

Eating in her new kitchen with Antonio felt surprisingly intimate. His presence seemed to fill the entire space and even seeped into the corners of her heart. She knew she'd miss him when he left, but it wasn't like she could keep him hostage here. He had a life in San Francisco, and she had a life here.

When they finished eating, Antonio said, "Which room can I start unpacking?"

"You don't have to keep working," Jo said. "You've already done all the heavy-lifting since you showed up."

He eyed her, then looked to the small living room. "How about I unpack the boxes for the living room, then we'll call it a night."

"All right." Jo stifled a yawn. He'd be leaving first thing in the morning, and the place would be far from finished, but that was all right. She'd get to everything eventually.

He headed into the living room and began to load books into the bookcases that he'd carried in earlier that day. Jo unpacked the final box of kitchen supplies. She'd have to get rid of a few things since she didn't have room for all the baking implements she'd collected over the years. Dang. She'd donated everything she felt like she could part with.

"What's this?" Antonio's voice cut into her thoughts.

She turned to find him in the doorway between the kitchen and the living room. He held her binder that contained her research notes for her Mongol queen's book. A second binder was somewhere in those boxes—her first fifty or so drafted pages.

Pasted on the front was a piece of paper with "Research for my first book" written across it in red letters.

"Oh, that." She shrugged. "Something I've worked on for a few years. I was going to finish writing this summer, but then Maggie invited me on her trip, and . . . Well, you know the rest."

Antonio's brow had furrowed, and he opened the binder and flipped through it. "These are just notes. Where's the book?"

Jo released a laugh. "Uh, good question. I've written a few chapters. They're in another binder."

He turned and headed to the living room. Jo realized what he was going to do.

"No, you don't," she said, hurrying after him.

But it was too late. He'd rummaged through the box and found the second binder. And yep, across the cover, it read: "My first book."

Cheesy, she knew, but it had been kind of exhilarating to write.

"Wait." She knelt by his side and tugged the binder from his hands, then pressed it against her chest. "It's not finished."

Antonio's dark eyes connected with hers. "That's okay. Can I read some of it?"

She tilted her head. "No."

His gaze moved over her face. "I could read what you have so far."

She looked down at the binder. "It's a mess, really."

"I don't mind." His voice was low, husky, and she raised her gaze to meet his.

"Why are you so interested?"

"Why wouldn't I be interested in something you wrote?"

Because Liam never asked her a thing about her book. Jo pushed that thought away. "It's about the Mongol queens, and probably needs a lot of revision before it sees the light of day. That is, after I finish the book."

With his gaze steady on her, Antonio reached out and wrapped his fingers around the binder, then gently tugged it from her. For some reason, Jo relaxed her grasp.

As he opened it and read the first page, she bit her lip. What was he thinking? What was he about to say?

He flipped a page, and Jo folded her arms tightly. He kept reading. Another page, and another. At the end of the first chapter, he looked up. "It's good, *cara*. Interesting." He started to read chapter two, but Jo tugged the binder back onto her lap.

"That's enough," she said, trying to say it in a firm tone.

"I don't know why you're hiding it," Antonio said. "When will you have it finished?"

Jo gave a half-laugh. "I don't know. I wanted to finish it two years ago in the summer, but I could never really focus. Summer is when I have more time. Then everything in my life fell apart with the divorce . . ."

Antonio set his large hand over hers. "You've had a lot going on. I get it. But you should finish it now."

"Now?" Jo echoed.

"Yes, take a sabbatical," he said. "Finish your book. Teaching will always be there when you're done with the book."

The Healing Summer

Jo stared at him.

"What? Haven't you ever heard of a sabbatical?"

"I've heard of it, but not to . . ."

"Write a book?"

She nodded.

Antonio drew her hand toward him and pressed a kiss on her wrist. "I think you need a sabbatical. Your story is good, and I wouldn't be surprised if you have more than one publisher interested once it's finished. And there's always university presses who'd be very interested in a research masterpiece."

Jo tried not to gape. Was this man some sort of literary expert? "I thought you were an art dealer."

The edge of Antonio's mouth lifted. "I'm also on the board for the San Francisco Literary Advocates. And I read a lot, too." He leaned close. "At least think about it. A sabbatical would give you more time to travel—you know, visit San Francisco."

"Oh, I see where you're going with this," Jo teased. He was close enough to kiss now, so she did.

Antonio drew her in tight and kissed her again. His hands found their way into her hair, and she nearly melted into him.

"I don't think you see where I'm going with this, or you might be running the other direction," he whispered.

Jo lifted a hand and ran her fingers over the scruff of his jaw. "It's probably a good thing to keep me in the dark, then."

He brushed his mouth against her fingers, and she looped her arms about his neck.

"At least think about it. You know it sounds prestigious when you say that you're on a sabbatical."

Jo had to laugh at that. "You're one of a kind, Antonio Gallo."

Chapter Twenty-Seven

JO COULDN'T REMEMBER THE last time she'd had a full night's sleep. It certainly wasn't in the past week, and it certainly wouldn't be tonight. She was wide awake at one in the morning, staring at the patchwork of light on the ceiling coming from the streetlamp outside her condo.

Maggie had called her earlier that day and told her if she ever decided to take a sabbatical, then she was always welcome to the extra bedroom in the bungalow. But that would put her in very close proximity to Antonio and his entire family. That felt . . . too much of everything.

And she had responsibilities in Seattle.

Today, she'd gone to the university and jumped into a couple of faculty meetings. Everyone had been nice to her like they always were, but there was still a distance there. Liam had been everyone's favorite.

Jo sighed and turned over. At her feet, Sadie shifted on the bed.

"You can't sleep, either, girl?" Jo asked. In a moment, a wet nose nudged her shoulder, and Jo wrapped her arm around her lug of a dog. "I miss him. That will fade, right?"

Sadie didn't answer.

"You're no help," Jo said and burrowed into the dog's fur.

Somehow, she fell asleep, but when she awakened a few hours later, her neck was sore. She peeled herself off the bed, grabbed a glass of water from the kitchen, and took a couple of ibuprofen. Sadie padded in after her.

"What's wrong, girl?" Jo asked, looking into her dog's mournful eyes.

Sadie nudged her head against Jo's leg, and she reached down to scratch the dog's head.

"I still miss him." Jo sighed. "How long will this go on? Another week? Two weeks?"

Here she was talking in the kitchen to herself—well, technically, to Sadie.

Jo headed to the phone and called Alec like she had been doing every morning before school. Their conversations were short, but they always gave her a boost.

"Hi, Mom," Alec said, his voice coming through loud and clear.

Jo smiled. "Hi, heading to school soon?"

"Yep, and I'm trying out for the soccer team today," he said.

"Oh, wow." Her son hadn't ever seemed interested in athletics. "What brought this on?"

"My friends are trying out, and they say that I'm good enough to make it," he said. "It's club, so they play in the fall. Then if I'm good enough, I could make the middle school team in the spring. That would be totally rad."

Jo loved the enthusiasm in his voice. "That's great, hon. I'm excited to hear how it goes."

"If I make it, can you come to my games?"

She inhaled. "When are they?" She couldn't jump on a plane every weekend.

"I don't know," Alec said. "I haven't made the team. Gotta go, Mom."

"Okay, bye, son."

He was off the phone, and she sat at the kitchen table. Her son was becoming his own person, trying new things. Without her. Jo rubbed her sore neck. Emotions washed over her, and well, she wished Antonio was here. He'd know what to say. She could call him, but she knew what he'd say. *If you lived closer, you could go to more games.*

It was true, too.

Jo gazed at the phone, thinking. What if . . . what if she called the dean of the history department and discussed a sabbatical? Maybe she could start it next semester. That wouldn't help with the soccer games in the fall, but if Alec was on the middle school team in the spring . . . What was she thinking? Was she really considering moving, again?

Jo picked up the phone and dialed before she could change her mind. If she didn't ask, she'd never know if there were options. Mr. Rudy answered on the third ring, sounding out of breath.

"Hi, Bill, it's Jo," she said. "Do you have a minute to talk?"

"Sure, I just got in," he said. "Velma isn't even here yet."

Velma was the department secretary.

She heard some shuffling on the other end.

"Okay, shoot. What's up?"

"I'm, uh, thinking of taking a sabbatical winter semester," Jo blurted out.

When Bill didn't say anything right away, she continued, explaining about her son having moved to San Diego with Liam, and how she'd spent part of the summer in San Francisco, helping with an art gallery, and how if she took a sabbatical, she could finish up her book. She told him she was thinking of moving to San Francisco, and being only a short plane trip from San Diego when she needed to visit her son. When she finished, she felt out of breath.

And Bill hadn't said a word.

"Of course, I can work in trips to San Diego on the weekends. Maybe have someone cover a Friday here and there." She squeezed her eyes shut. Was Bill upset?

"Jo, I had no idea all of this was going on," he said at last. "Why didn't you say something?"

"I guess . . . I didn't really know how to mix personal stuff with work."

"I've heard you talk about the research for your book for years, and I agree that it needs to be finished. It will be a valuable contribution." He paused. "You do know that we have an affiliation program in San Francisco, right?"

Jo wracked her mind. Did she know? On one level, she knew the university had affiliation programs. "It sounds familiar."

"I could talk to the dean of the history department and see what their needs are," he said. "But regardless, you can take a sabbatical. There are three applications on my desk right now from over the summer."

Jo blinked. "Really?" Her mind began to race. In January, she might be moving to San Francisco.

"I don't see why you couldn't start right way," he said. "One of the applicants called me yesterday, inquiring again, saying that he was available this semester. Even if it was as a substitute."

Jo exhaled. This was not what she expected. She couldn't think straight. "I don't know what to say," she said with a half-laugh. "I thought . . ."

"How about I call the dean right now and see if I can get ahold of him," Bill said. "As far as I'm concerned, you have your sabbatical, and it can start this semester. The question is, which university will you return to after it's finished?"

When Jo hung up with Bill, she was stunned. Had it really

been that easy? She had her sabbatical... She released a shaky breath. Covering her face with her hands, she tried to comprehend all that Bill had said. As of now, she could leave. The thought was both terrifying and exhilarating. Moving to San Francisco would put her in close proximity to Antonio. And taking a sabbatical would mean really immersing herself in the project she'd been dragging with her for years.

She was still at the kitchen table when the phone rang again. Her heart nearly stopped. Picking up the receiver, she said, "Hello?"

"Jo, it's Bill," he said in a rushed voice. "Just got off the phone with your replacement during your sabbatical. Peter Jensen is thrilled, even though I said it's only a one-year contract. But that brings me to my first phone call. Dennis Stevens is at the history department of Angelo. He said he'd definitely be interested in a bright faculty member joining them next fall."

Jo blinked back the emotion filling her eyes. It was all coming together. Just like that. But she had this lease on her condo, and so many other things to consider, such as . . . Nothing else came to mind.

Her husband was gone, her son was gone, her house was gone . . .

"All right," she said, her voice trembling. "I'll take the sabbatical. And if you give me Mr. Stevens's number, I'll give him a call."

The smile in Bill's voice was plain. "Good for you. It's about time you got the long end of the stick, Jo. You've been an asset to our program for years, yet you don't always get recognition for your work. You deserve to finish this book of yours, and I can't wait to read it when you're done."

Jo was both smiling and crying. "Thank you," she whispered.

Bill said a few other things, but Jo barely comprehended them. When she hung up, she knelt next to Sadie and gave her a fierce hug. "We're moving, girl. I don't know how this all happened, but it's happening."

Sadie thumped her tail.

"Right? I think I need to call Maggie. We're going to need a place to stay."

The morning was still early, but Jo dialed Maggie's number. Her scratchy voice answered, and Jo spilled out the whole story without stopping to take a breath.

"Goodness," Maggie said. "Am I dreaming?"

Jo laughed. "If you are, then I am, too."

Her voice lowered. "Have you told Antonio?"

"No," Jo said, her heart rising to her throat. "I wanted to run it past you first. You know, since I'll need a place to stay until I can figure everything else out."

"You'd better call him now, dear—this news shouldn't wait another moment."

When Jo hung up with Maggie, she took a few moments to collect her thoughts. Antonio had brought up the subject over and over, but what if the reality wasn't as appealing?

She picked up the phone again, then glanced at Sadie. "Here goes nothing, girl."

When Antonio's deep voice answered, she felt a warm burst of goose bumps across her skin.

"Hi," she said.

"Good morning, *cara*."

The affection in that short phrase bolstered her courage. "I got the sabbatical, and I'm coming to San Francisco."

"What? Are you serious?" His voice was full of wonder and laughter.

She grinned. "I am. Maggie said I could stay with her until I figure out things."

"I can book the next flight and help you—"

"No," Jo cut in. "You've done so much already. Keep an eye out for a woman driving a blue car, and a dog in the front seat."

Antonio chuckled.

And that was how, four days later, Jo found herself driving up the long driveway to the Gallo estate. It turned out that she'd found a sub-leaser through a friend of Bill's, and not having unpacked much was to her advantage. The moving truck would be a couple of days behind her. But for now, she drove along the treelined driveway, expecting the Gallo home to come into view at any moment.

And when it did, there was a man standing at the top of the driveway. His dark hair waving to his collar, his hands in the pockets of his dress slacks, his gaze intent on the arriving car.

Antonio.

She parked, exhaling a shaky breath as all kinds of butterflies danced in her stomach. By the time she climbed out of the car, and Sadie bounded past her, Antonio was already walking toward her.

This time, he didn't pause to greet Sadie. Instead, his eyes were solely on her. Those beautiful, dark eyes that were warm and often amused at the same time.

"How did you know I was arriving at this very moment?" she asked.

He closed the distance of the last two steps between them. "I just knew." He cradled her face in his hands and kissed her. Softly. "I love you, *cara*. Welcome home."

Her eyes fluttered closed as he kissed her again.

Was this what home felt like?

"Jo!" a woman exclaimed from the porch. *Stella.*

Antonio didn't release her, and he didn't stop kissing her.

Not when his mother showed up, and not when Maggie showed up. He had no problem kissing her in front of everyone who came out to greet her. Antonio Gallo style.

Epilogue

DEAR ORLANDO,

I haven't written since early summer in my journal. There is so much to say. I've found you again, and the miracles continue from roping my neighbor Jo Sampson into coming to San Francisco and searching one last time for you. Jo found your family, and now I'm living in the bungalow on your estate.

The events that brought me here are both a dream and a miracle.

You won't believe all that has happened, or maybe you do believe. Maybe you're watching from wherever you are. I hope you can. The gallery is coming along. We had a grand opening, but I'm constantly fussing, and rearranging things. I want everything perfect. For you. Because you deserve your work showcased and never forgotten.

Just as you never forgot me, I never forgot you.

I still remember that moment that your great-niece, Stella, led me into the studio you'd named after me. Even now, it's hard to comprehend, to believe.

Our time together was so short, yet it impacted both of our lives forever.

Yours still impacts mine.

When I wake in the morning to the sunrise, I think of all the sunrises you saw. When I walk among the garden paths of your estate, I think of the steps you must have taken. And finally, when I look upon your paintings, I remember. Just as you intended, I remember and believe.

I love you, Orlando. I always will.

I can only hope that providence will bring us together once again in another lifetime.

Now, I must write later. I have a wedding to attend. One in the garden, between Jo and Antonio.

We are celebrating so many things this fall. Jo is back to working on her manuscript, and Antonio finally let us see his art. Beautiful landscape paintings full of color, vibrancy, and life. He's letting me put two of them in the gallery. Just where they belong.

You will continue to be in our hearts, and I can't wait to see your great-nephew and my best friend marry.

The day is beautiful, and their love even more beautiful.

Love always,

Maggie

Heather B. Moore is a *USA Today* bestselling author of more than seventy publications. Her historical novels and thrillers are written under pen name H.B. Moore. She writes women's fiction, romance, and inspirational non-fiction under Heather B. Moore. This can all be confusing, so her kids just call her Mom. Heather attended Cairo American College in Egypt, the Anglican School of Jerusalem in Israel, and earned a Bachelor of Science degree from Brigham Young University. Heather is represented by Dystel, Goderich, and Bourret.

For book updates, sign up for Heather's email list: hbmoore.com/contact

Website: HBMoore.com
Facebook: Fans of H. B. Moore
Blog: MyWritersLair.blogspot.com
Instagram: @authorhbmoore
Twitter: @HeatherBMoore

www.ingramcontent.com/pod-product-compliance
Lightning Source LLC
LaVergne TN
LVHW021811060526
838201LV00058B/3322